PUFFIN BOOKS

Napper's Big Match

After the brilliant success of the Red Row ~~~ ~~~
Primary Schools League, most of the team move up to the
big school. Only Napper and Daniel Rooney are left, and
Mr Hope, Red Row's head, can't help them form another
team.

Napper is determined to find a team to play for, and
Coldwater Reserves sound promising; but his first game is
very rough and things begin to look bad. Out of the blue,
however, Napper's big chance comes along.

Follow the fortunes of Napper McCann, Demon Goalscorer,
in this fantastic new story, the fourth in the series.

Martin Waddell has played football nearly all his life, and
as a teenager was an apprentice goalkeeper for Fulham. He
was born and educated in Northern Ireland and has written
a great number of books, both for children and adults. He
also writes under the pen-name Catherine Sefton, and many
of these titles have Irish settings. He lives in County Down
with his wife and three sons.

Martin Waddell

Napper's Big Match

Illustrated by Michael Strand

Puffin Books

For Jamie Wright, my 'best reader'

PUFFIN BOOKS

Published by the Penguin Group
Penguin Books Ltd, 27 Wrights Lane, London w8 5tz, England
Penguin Books USA Inc., 375 Hudson Street, New York, New York 10014, USA
Penguin Books Australia Ltd, Ringwood, Victoria, Australia
Penguin Books Canada Ltd, 10 Alcorn Avenue, Toronto, Ontario, Canada m4v 3b2
Penguin Books (NZ) Ltd, 182–190 Wairau Road, Auckland 10, New Zealand

Penguin Books Ltd, Registered Offices: Harmondsworth, Middlesex, England

First published 1993
10 9 8 7 6 5 4 3 2 1

Printed in England by Clays Ltd, St Ives plc
Filmset in Baskerville

Contents

Top Row (L. to R.): M. Bellow, Miss Fellows, Mr Hope, T. Prince, H. Brown

Middle Row: P. Scott, A. Watts, H. Haxwell, D. King, J. Deacon, J. Small, D. Rooney, S. Rodgers

Bottom Row: D. Forbes, C. Small, N. McCann, E. Boomer, D. Wilson, J. Ramsey

1. Falling Stars

This should be a picture of the new Red Row Stars team taking over from the World Famous Great Brilliant Red Row Stars Team of the Century, captained by Demon Goalscorer Super Star Napper McCann, but it isn't. It is a picture of what we had left after half the team – all the big ones – went to their new schools.

That was what we thought we had left when school started again in September. Then big Marky Bellow said he wasn't going to play in a team that was no good because everyone was small and Scottie Watts started Scouts on Saturday mornings and Dribbler Wilson broke his arm fishing.

'No team this year, boys,' Mr Hope said. 'We haven't got enough players to make it worthwhile running one.'

'Helena Bellow could play,' I said. 'She is as good as old Marky any day!'

'We still wouldn't have enough,' Mr Hope said.

Daniel Rooney and I thought he was saying it because he didn't want to give up his Saturday mornings to go with the team. He said we could still have practice matches amongst ourselves on Wednesdays after school and he would coach us, and maybe next year we would have enough good players to make up a team.

'We won't be here next year!' I told him.

'I can't materialize footballers out of thin air, just to suit you two, Napper!' he said.

'If we can't be in a league this year, maybe we could play some friendlies?' Daniel suggested.

That was the way the original Stars started, with friendlies, and everybody said we couldn't have a team but we did and it was brilliant.

'Well, maybe,' Mr Hope said, but it sounded like, *Maybe not*.

'Mr Hope is right,' Daniel said, when we were on our way home. 'We wouldn't have much of a team, would we? All the other schools have packs of big players and we would be putting out P4s against them. We would be beaten all the time, and then the P4s wouldn't want to play. Or they would get kicked to bits and their mothers would come in and shout at Mr Hope.'

'He's just too lazy to run it this year,' I said.

I was annoyed with Mr Hope. Daniel and I could have made our team good, but he wouldn't give us the chance. We might not have won as many games as the old Red Row Stars, but we would still have had our own team.

We took our ball out on the Common anyway and played One-Two-Pass-Bang, which is one of the games Mr Hope taught us to make training more interesting.

This is how to do it:

The idea is to one-touch pass using the line of sticks as defenders. Whoever receives the ball after the last defender has to shoot for goal, and the other player has to control the ball when it comes back, make a turn and pass, so they begin all over again. It looks very simple, but it is difficult.

Mr Hope always made us start very slowly, just walking, and then gradually speed up.

We got fed up doing that so we had shots at goal. I got fifteen and Daniel got thirteen, so I won, but he said I didn't because of moving the posts and we were too tired for a penalty shoot-out, so I said it was a win and he said it was a draw. It wasn't much use practising when we had no team to play for any more because our manager didn't think we were good enough.

'We should be able to join some team,' Daniel said. 'We don't know enough people who are free on Saturdays to make our own team, but there are dozens of Youth Leagues. There must be billions and trillions of teams that we can play for.'

We thought a bit, and then Daniel said: 'Only we don't know anyone in them.'

'Doesn't matter,' I said. 'We'll be all right, once they see what we can do on the pitch.'

I thought that that was probably right. Daniel is a good player, though he fades out of the game sometimes, and I can play a bit.

That is what I told Boxer Lewis.

Boxer has a coffee stall down the Market. Eddie Boomer's mum goes there, and Eddie told her we had no team to play for. She told Eddie to tell us that Boxer ran one and he was looking for players.

'G-R-E-A-T!' I said.

'What team is it?' Daniel asked.

'Coldwater Reserves,' Eddie said. 'Zaniger League, Division Two.'

We were all set to sign on for Coldwater Reserves and play in the Zaniger League and we reckoned we wouldn't be in the Reserves long because we would break through into the First Team and be stars all over again, just like at school. So we went to see Boxer Lewis at his stall. We told him we were footballers and we wanted a trial for his team, Coldwater Reserves.

'Dunno,' Boxer said.

He was huge, about six foot six, all legs and arms and broken nose. He wore a big yellow jersey with flowers on it that was really naff, and a yellow knitted hat with 'Mother' written on it in red letters.

'We can play a bit,' I told him. 'We played in the Barnleck and District.'

Miss Fellows made a mistake and put Red Row Stars in the Barnleck and District, and some of the teams gave us a really tough time, but we didn't tell Boxer that. It was before we had our Red Row Stars team properly organized and we were up against lots of big players, so it proved we weren't too small to play for Coldwater Reserves, which is what we thought he might say.

'Dunno,' he said.

He had to go and serve somebody a Giant Burger and then he came back.

'You at Red Row School like Eddie was?' he said.

'Yes,' Daniel said.

'Still at it?' he said.

We both nodded, trying to look big, because we could guess what he was thinking from the way he spoke.

'Primary School, ain't it?' he said. 'Big blokes in the Zaniger would walk all over you. Youth League it is, not for little kids.'

'Just give us a trial,' I said.

'Dunno,' he said. 'No use, is it? I mean, look at you!'

'How can you know it is no use, when you *haven't* looked at us?' I said. 'You haven't seen us play. Eddie's mum told us you need players and you keep losing and you are bottom of the league.'

Maybe it wasn't the right thing to say, but it was what Eddie Boomer's mum had told Eddie to tell us.

'Naff off!' Boxer said.

I was really annoyed. I wasn't going to *naff off* and lose the one chance we had of making it into a real team.

'Do you hold training sessions?' I asked.

'Yeah,' he said. 'Tuesdays, down the Neck.'

'Well, can we come to your training?' I said.

'Because we have to find some team to play for and we won't play well if we haven't been training. Then you can see what we can do.'

'Dunno,' he said. 'No point, is there?'

'Absolutely no point,' Daniel said, when we were on our way home.

'We go to their training and there is bound to be a kick-about and we'll get playing,' I said. 'He thinks we are too small to be any good in his team, but we can show him he's wrong.'

I wanted to show Mr Hope *he* was wrong too. He could have had a good team still at Red Row, even with the little ones in it, because Daniel and I could have *made* it good. I thought if we signed on for a big team and got goals, then everybody would know he was wrong chucking Red Row Stars in, and it would make Mr Hope look silly.

'I don't think I'll bother,' Daniel said.

'Try it,' I said. 'Just once.'

'No, Napper,' Daniel said. 'Coldwater Reserves must be a dumb team if Boxer is their coach, and he doesn't want us to go down there anyway, you know that.'

'All he said was "dunno",' I said. 'And we have more chance of getting a game if it isn't a very good team!'

'I would rather wait and find a good team,' Daniel said.

'They'll be a good team if they have us playing for them,' I said.

Daniel humped up his shoulders and took a kick at a can that was lying on the ground. 'Pass?' he said, and he played it towards me.

I let it go.

I was *serious*.

I know the Neck. There are some tough kids down that way, and I didn't want to go there by myself. I wanted Daniel with me, first time, even if he didn't want to come.

I told him he was chicken. He started mumbling about Eddie Boomer. He said Eddie shouldn't have sent us down to a no-hope kickers' team.

'That is more or less what Eddie *is*,' I said. 'A no-hope kicker. You are better than Eddie. You *and* me. We'll show them.'

'I'm not going,' Daniel said.

He thought that was it, but I fixed him.

I got into school early the next morning and I went around telling everyone that Daniel and I had got a trial for Coldwater Reserves in the Zaniger League, Division Two, and they were all chuffed.

'That is really brilliant, Napper!' Helena Bellow said. 'I bet you and Daniel both get selected for the team.'

'I bet you come a cropper!' Ugly Irma Bank-

worth said, and after that there was no way
Daniel could back out of it.

I wasn't *lying*. It *was* a trial for Coldwater
Reserves, sort of, or I thought it would be if
we could get in their kick-about. I would
smash in some Napper McCann Super Star
goals and make old Boxer eat his droopy
'Mother' hat.

'Best of luck, Napper!' Mr Hope said, but I
thought he didn't mean it.

If he had meant it he would have let us have
our own school team instead of deciding he was
too busy to run it.

We would show him we were Super Stars
and he was w-r-o-n-g!

2. Coldwater Reserves: Training

'It's getting dark!' Daniel said. 'I don't like the look of this!'

He was right.

We were down the Neck with our kit in our bags and it was twenty-past seven. Training for Coldwater Reserves was supposed to start at half-past.

'How can we play if it is dark?' Daniel said. 'I told you we should have stayed home.'

'Dunno,' I said, trying to make a joke of it by sounding like Boxer, but I was feeling choked. It looked as if Boxer thought it would be funny to let us turn up at the Neck after dark, when he knew nobody would be there.

The Neck is a tough place. It isn't the sort of place I'd go walking about after dark, usually.

Then . . .

'There they are!' I shouted. 'There's the pitch!'

'Some pitch!' Daniel said.

It was one of those cage enclosures, with tiny seven-a-side goals and half a dozen lights.

'Is that the Coldwater Reserves team?' Daniel asked.

I didn't think it could be. They had no ball or kit, and they didn't look like footballers, but . . .

'Don't see anybody else,' I said.

'Those aren't kids,' Daniel said.

'Yeah,' I said. 'Can't be them.'

Then three kids came up. They were bigger than us, but they could have been thirteen or fourteen. They had a ball. One of them booted it over the wire and they all ran into the cage shouting.

'That must be them,' I said.

Daniel made a face. He was thinking what I was thinking. They all looked big and tough.

'Let's go in,' I said, because there wasn't any point in hanging about. If they were going to play football, I was going to play football. That was what I'd come down to the Neck to do.

'Wait till Boxer comes,' Daniel said unhappily. 'We don't know them, do we?'

So we waited.

I didn't like it. I would much rather have been in there, banging the ball about and getting the feel of it before the training started, but I didn't want to go in there on my own, and Daniel wouldn't.

A big fat kid with a whistle and track suit came trotting down to the cage.

He stood in the gate and blew his whistle. Then he started shouting, but the kids in the cage – there were about a dozen by now, all *bigger* than us – didn't take any notice of him.

'Shut up, Dicey!' one of them yelled, and he belted the ball at the fat kid. The fat kid caught it one-handed, the way Mr Hope says Pat Jennings used to do it.

Here is Dicey doing it:

'Did you see that?' Daniel said, sounding very impressed.

Dicey threw the ball back, straight as an arrow. He was so quick making the throw that the big kid who had chucked it couldn't control it, and Dicey shouted at him and laughed.

'Good catch!' Daniel said. 'Brilliant throw.'

'He could have caught two-handed,' I said. 'That is just showing off.'

It was the sort of catch that looks good in training, but often goes wrong in a game. Showy goalies are usually the ones who make mistakes in the end, because they think more about making the save look good than making the save.

'He had his whistle in his other hand,' Daniel pointed out. Maybe he was right. It was a good one-hander, but I reckoned if he had tried it in a match he might have dropped it and then Demon Goalscorer N. McCann would have nipped in and scored another Wonder Goal.

I was fed up just standing there, so I went up to the kid with the whistle.

'Mister?' I said. I didn't know what to call him so I called him Mister. He looked big enough to be a Mister. I thought he was probably their trainer or something. The Coldwater First's Trainer that is. Boxer Lewis trained the Reserve team that we were trying to get into.

'Yeah?'

'Is this the Coldwater Football Team Training?' I asked.

'Who's asking?' he said, which was silly, because he could see who was asking. Well, he wasn't looking at us, so I suppose he couldn't, but he must have seen us waiting by the cage.

'We're footballers,' I said. 'Boxer said we could come down and train with the Coldwater Reserves Football Team, so is this it?'

'Boxer?' he said. 'Where is he?'

'Don't know,' I said. 'He said we could come down.'

'What for?'

I took a deep breath.

'So we could get in the team,' I said.

'What team?' he said. He didn't answer my questions. He just kept asking questions of his own. He wasn't interested in us at all. He had a scrubby bit of paper with names on, and he was putting ticks and crosses against the names, checking out who was there and who wasn't.

He stopped his name-ticking and looked at me.

'Who is going to change your nappies at half-time?' he said, and he grinned all over his face, as though he thought he had said something very funny. 'Naff off,' he added, and he went into the cage, closing the gate behind him.

'That's it, Napper,' Daniel said. 'That is twice

20

we've been told to naff off, so I'm doing it!' And he picked up his bag and slung it over his shoulder.

'Get stripped!' I said.

'What?'

'We came down here to show them we could play football and that is what we're going to do,' I said. I was mad. They were playing football in the cage and their coach wouldn't even pay us any attention. He just wanted to make *stupid* jokes about changing our nappies.

Daniel hesitated.

'Nobody else is,' he said. 'Stripped, I mean. It's Tarmac, that is. I don't want my legs cut up.'

'Then just get in there,' I said.

I shoved him in through the cage gate.

If I hadn't shoved him, I think he would have gone home without even trying.

'You going to let us play?' I shouted at Dicey.

'You want to play?' he shouted back. 'OK! You play. You risk your necks. Don't blame me if you go home with a pair of broken legs apiece!'

Nobody told us what side to play on, so we decided to play on the one that was kicking into Dicey's goal.

Nobody would pass to us. They didn't pass much anyway. They were dashing about, banging into each other, chasing the ball and shouting. We decided we would get the ball and pass to each other!

Daniel hadn't really wanted to play, but he made up for it by chasing after the ball, hunting for it. He would have got it, but one of their players ran straight at him and barged into him sending him crashing into the cage wire.

Daniel got up looking furious, but the player who had crashed him just laughed. Then it was my turn. I went in to tackle a big kid called Mort. He had gone for a high ball and he was trying to control it, but he was the kind of player who couldn't control a rice pudding. The ball hit his knee and broke away from him and the next minute I was on it and heading for the goal with Dicey in it.

One of them came across and went at me, but I jinked him and turned inside. Then I could see Dicey coming off his line and I thought I would feint for the right corner and then nick it low down to his left for a Napper McCann Super Star tap-in goal that would make him look silly.

That's what I thought.

Here's what happened:

'PENALTY!' someone yelled.

'No flaming penalty. He's not in the flaming team!' Mort shouted.

There were three of us lying all tangled up in a pile in the goal circle.

'You could have killed the kid, Dicey!'

'This is a team practice! Who let those kids on?'

'Dicey did.'

'No I didn't,' Dicey said. 'They let themselves on. They asked for it.'

'I'm going to kick this one off!' Mort said, grabbing me by the shoulder.

'Dunno about that!' somebody said.

It was Boxer.

He'd turned up late, but better late than never.

'I dunno,' he repeated slowly. 'Penalty, I reckon.'

He picked the ball up, and put it on the edge of the circle, ready for the kick.

'Anybody want to argue?' he asked.

'He's not supposed to be playing,' Mort muttered, massaging the back of his neck where Boxer had grabbed him.

'Dunno,' said Boxer. 'He looked to me as if he was playing.'

'OK! OK!' Dicey said, starting to grin. 'OK, Boxer! Penalty it is. Right! Sure thing. Only I'm in goal, and the kid has to take it!'

'Yeah! Yeah! Yeah!' they all started shouting.

They thought it was funny.

They thought I would muck it up.

Dicey thought it was his big chance to show off what a brilliant keeper he was. He started playing about. He wasn't that big, but he was big enough, and the goal wasn't. First he pretended that he was going to lie down across the goal waving his arms, and then he didn't. He stretched himself out with his legs wide apart, wagging his arms and making ape faces at me.

'Come on!' Dicey shouted. 'Pick your spot!'

Daniel came up to me.

'He won't be able to move much, with his feet like that,' Daniel said. 'Try planting it in the corner.'

I thought that might have been all right, but Dicey had arms like an octopus, and he was a real goalie when he wasn't mucking about. I thought he might be able to save my shot if I went for the corner, unless I was spot-on accurate.

'Don't keep us all night!' Dicey shouted.

I walked back from the ball and turned. I knew exactly what I was going to do.

Five paces forward and . . . WHAM!

Right through his legs!

By mucking about and standing on his goal-line almost doing the splits, Dicey was hopelessly

off balance. He couldn't get his legs together quickly enough to stop the ball. It wouldn't have worked with a goalie like Dicey in a big goal, because the spot kick would have been taken from further away, and he would have had time to readjust his body. It wouldn't have worked in a small one either, if he hadn't mucked about, or if I hadn't managed to place it exactly.

Another N. McCann Wonder Goal, in my first-ever game at Coldwater!

'GOAL!' all my team shouted, and they started mucking about and laughing at Dicey.

He'd gone over on his back trying to close his legs quickly, and he didn't like it.

He hooked the ball out of the net, and booted it . . . straight at *us*. It didn't get me, but it got Daniel, and Daniel went down as if he had been pole-axed.

That was the end of the training.

I had to help Daniel after Boxer got him off, and anyway I didn't want to play any more.

'Are they your team?' I asked Boxer, because I didn't see how they could be. Most of them looked about sixteen.

'No,' he said. 'Just what turned up. Some of my lot and some of the Firsts, and some who just happened to be here. I'm lucky if I get eleven on a Saturday. Most of the Seconds don't come down the Neck. It gets a bit rough, sometimes.'

'Yeah,' Daniel said. 'It does, doesn't it?'

'What about Saturday?' I said. 'Have you got a game?'

'Friendly,' he said. 'Down Starrett, against Dixon Sports.'

'Right,' I said. 'I'll bring my boots.'

He looked at me.

'Dunno,' he said. 'Might as well. Might be one short.' He stopped and had a long think about it, and then he said, 'You *can* play a bit.'

'You mean . . . I'm picked?'

'I didn't mean you can play against Dixon,' he said. 'That is one game we want to win, this time. I meant, you *can* play. Good spot kick. Good run. Just haven't got the weight, have you?' Then he went off.

'You going down Starrett, Saturday?' Daniel said.

'Yes,' I said.

'I'm not,' said Daniel. His leg was all bruises where he'd crashed into the cage, and he was limping.

'That was the First team,' I said. 'Some of it. They weren't even trying to play football. The Reserves are in Division Two. Our size almost. It'll be different.'

'Boxer is not going to give you a game,' Daniel said. 'Didn't you listen? If he did, you'd get knocked all over the shop. All you'll be doing is watching.'

'Well, I'll turn up until I do get a game against someone or until I find another team to play for,' I said.

'Rather you than me,' Daniel said.

At the time I thought he might be right. I didn't know if I was going to get a game, because Boxer's 'dunno' didn't tell me anything. Daniel knew *he* wasn't, because he hadn't done anything, apart from being bundled into the wire once and hit with the ball the second time he got near it, so he had no chance. If I was going to make it into a new football team I had to go solo and make the best of any opportunity

I had to start playing. That's how I ended up heading for Starrett Common on my own on Saturday, all ready for my brilliant début in the match between Coldwater Reserves and Dixon Sports. Someone mightn't turn up and I might play after all!

3. Coldwater Reserves v. Dixon Sports

UNDER-14 FRIENDLY
Coldwater Reserves v. Dixon Sports
Referee: B. Lewis (Unofficial)
Venue: Pitch 7, Starrett Common, Starrett

I got a game all right, but it wasn't for Coldwater Reserves, Boxer Lewis's team. It was against them.

I'd been hoping that Coldwater Reserves were so disorganized that half their team wouldn't turn up and I would get on, but it didn't work out like that. Their First-team game was cancelled, and some of the First-team players came along wanting a game, so there was no room for me.

'Maybe next week, kid,' Boxer Lewis said to me, and I was left standing on the touch-line with my boots, wishing I hadn't come. Then Dixon Sports came. They had a blue and white minibus with 'Dixon Sports FC' on the side and a kit hamper and a blue and white painted medical box that their trainer carried, but they had only nine players.

Their manager, Harry somebody or other, hopped out of the minibus and came over to Boxer Lewis.

'Sorry, pal,' he said, 'but some of our lads had to go for a trial down at Owen Lane, the new community thingy. Their stand-ins didn't make it, so we are down to nine.'

'Tough,' Boxer said, grinning.

'We thought you could lend us a sub or two to make up the numbers, seeing it is only a friendly.'

'Dunno,' Boxer said.

I couldn't see what he was 'dunno-ing' about, because he had at least four extra players standing around with their boots, but that is what he said. He went over and talked to his players. There seemed to be a lot of head-shaking going on.

When Boxer came back he said, 'We can let you have *him*,' and pointed at me.

'Him?' Harry said. 'He's only a kid.'

'Yeah, well, some of my lads are carrying injuries from the last time,' Boxer said, and he grinned. Some of the Coldwater players had come with him to hear the conversation, and they started laughing and joking about something, I don't know what.

'You want a game, son?' Harry asked me.

'Yeah! Brilliant!' I said.

Dixon Sports had already changed into their blue and white stripes and locked their minibus, so I went down to the dressing-room with the Coldwater players to change. It was a funny feeling, changing with the team I was playing against. Coldwater had their kit all rumpled up in a big floppy bag, and they chucked it at each other. The first thing I noticed was that the four who were First team, which is Under-16, were all picked to play. I wondered if Dixon Sports knew that Coldwater were putting on over-age players, but then I realized that it was only a friendly, not played under League rules, so that there wouldn't be anything they could do about it.

Coldwater didn't seem to be treating it like a friendly! They kept muttering to each other about getting something back for the last time, and teaching Dixon Sports' fancy team a lesson they wouldn't forget in a hurry.

I didn't ask anybody what the last time was. Nobody talked to me, and I talked to nobody. I got my things on and went out to the pitch.

'You playing for us?' a big kid they called Gus asked me, when I got there.

'Yes,' I said.

'How many games have you played for *them*?' he asked.

'None, yet,' I said. 'I'm on trial, sort of.'

'Yeah, I thought so!' he said, and he went over to Harry and started complaining.

'Typical Coldwater,' said Harry. 'They're out to get us because we put them out of the Cup. They won't be taking any prisoners.'

Harry came over to me. 'You look like you'll drown in that jersey, son,' he said.

It was a bit big.

'They've set you up, son,' he said. 'Are you sure you want to play? This could be a rough one.'

'Yes,' I said.

He looked doubtful. There were half a dozen Coldwater players who *weren't* playing, standing on the touch-line. If Coldwater had wanted to help Dixon Sports, some of them could have played.

'All turned up to see the grudge match!' he said. 'Pity they couldn't have loaned us a full-sized player or two, to make a game of it. No harm to you, son . . . but just you stay out on the wing and don't get kicked, OK?'

'Funny coincidence, how their First-team game got put off,' Gus said, 'just the day they were playing us.'

'Yeah,' Harry said. 'Coldwater coincidence!'

Then he went off to talk to Boxer about a referee. The referee was to have been organized by Coldwater, but no referee had turned up.

'Doesn't matter, if Harry gets the whistle,' the Dixon goalie said to Gus. The goalie looked the part. He had all the gear, cycling shorts beneath his football ones and knee-pads and gloves that were giant and flashy.

They tossed for ref and Boxer won.

'Double-headed coin, probably!' Gus muttered. The rest of the Dixon Sports team looked really down in the mouth.

It was a grudge match and the team I was playing for had only ten players and everybody on the field was bigger than me and now it

34

looked as if the referee might be dodgy as well. I decided I wasn't going to let it worry me. Nobody thought I could do anything, but then none of them had seen me play a proper match with N. McCann Wham-Bam Super Goals!

We lined up, and the Dixon striker, who was called Shotty, kicked off. He tapped it back, and they threaded it all the way back to the goalie, very coolly, as if they knew what they were doing.

The Coldwater players charged up the field.

The goalie didn't boot the ball aimlessly.

He yelled, 'Elie!' and threw it to the wing, where the back had pulled clear. Elie had the ball, and it was my side of the field. I started to move wide so that he would have room to run into, finding space for myself at the same time. But Elie didn't play it to me or run into the space I'd moved out of. Instead he waited until the Coldwater Number 10 wakened up and dashed on to him, and then he played it back to the keeper.

It seemed stupid to me.

We could have been off downfield.

'That's it! Let them do the running till we have things sorted!' Gus shouted. He was playing behind the back four and he seemed to be the Captain. The goalkeeper played a long ball downfield and Shotty went for it with the Number 5.

This is what I saw:

The whistle blasted.

Free kick to Dixon!

That's what I thought, and then I saw that the ref, Boxer Lewis, had given it the other way.

'Augh, ref!' Shotty complained, standing with his hands on his hips and glaring at Boxer.

'Making a back,' Boxer said.

'He came up *my* back!' Shotty said. He was going to keep on arguing but Gus yelled at him to keep clear of the ref.

It was a terrible decision of the ref's.

Making a back is when the attacking player backs into the defender just as he is about to jump. It is a really dangerous trick to play, because if it goes wrong the defender can be badly injured when he falls, like this:

That decision was bad enough, but the next one was worse.

We had only ten men, and Gus was telling his team to keep possession and contain Coldwater, making them run about by interpassing. He was hoping to tire Coldwater, and draw too many of them forward all at once, so that we could go suddenly for a break if the chance came. Gus was directing things and doing it cleverly and Coldwater weren't smart enough to see what was happening. They kept pounding after the ball, instead of trying to use their extra man to set up interceptions. Then our Number 8 got clear. He was going for a goal. Big Mort, who was supposed to be over marking me but had gone walkies because nobody was passing to me, cut across him. The Number 8 had played the ball forward, and Mort came crashing in so late that the ball had nothing to do with it.

CRUNCH.

Mort and the Number 8 went down in a bundle and the ball ran on to Dicey, who was another of the over-age ones that they had stuck on for their Revenge Match. Dicey got the ball and cleared it upfield, while all our players were waiting for the whistle to go.

'Hey! Boxer! Penalty!' Harry yelled from the touch-line.

Boxer just grinned at him and ran away.

'He's not going to give us *anything*!' Elie muttered, as he ran past me, covering back. 'Your lot are making sure of it, aren't they?'

I didn't like the way Coldwater were playing, crunching in for every ball, or the way *their* ref was reffing, and now it looked as if I was being blamed for it by the rest of the Dixon Sports team, just because I had turned up with Coldwater. The worst of it was I hadn't had a sniff of the ball.

I thought: get the ball and do something.

Elie got the ball, ignored me as usual, and played a long one upfield to Shotty. Shotty got the right side of the Number 5, skipped over the leg that was supposed to bring him down, and really lashed at the goal. It looked in the net all the way, but Dicey had come haring out of goal

38

and he somehow managed to get down and shove the ball to one side.

I was on my own, on the edge of the area.

Open goal!

BANG!

A Napper McCann Super Goal!

My first touch and it was in the back of the net and the Dixon players were leaping all over me and Harry was jumping up and down on the touch-line.

GOAL! GOAL! GOAL!

One touch and I'd done it!

The whistle went . . . for *offside*!

'Augh, ref!' I yelled.

I couldn't have been offside. I'd been coming from *behind* the ball, and anyway it had come off the keeper.

The whole Dixon Sports team went mad! They were all standing round Boxer shouting, but he just grinned and ran off upfield.

Then Mort came up to me.

'Don't you do that again, kiddo!' he said.

He put his hand out, as though he was going to ruffle my hair, being friendly, but instead he gripped my ear, and tugged.

'Oi!' I yelled.

Then Elie came running up, and got between us.

'Leave him alone,' Elie said, squaring up to Mort.

Pssst! Pssst! Pssst! went the whistle, and Boxer was over, reading Elie a lecture and threatening to send him off, when all Elie had been doing was stopping big Mort laying into me. Then Harry came on to the field and he started arguing with Boxer and in the end Boxer didn't give a free kick for offside. He gave a bounce ball where I'd been standing instead, which was ridiculous, because it was either a goal or it was offside.

'Good goal,' Elie said to me, when the game got going again, and he started passing to me, because he had realized that I wasn't just making up the numbers.

That should have been good, but Mort had got the same message.

Every time I got the ball he started coming at me, his arms going like windmills.

The first time Elie played the ball to me set the pattern. Mort came charging in. I knew he was going to lift me, ball or no ball, if I tried to turn, so I played the ball straight back to Elie and hopped over Mort's tackle. Mort slid along on the seat of his shorts, looking silly, with no chance at all of getting back to cover Elie as we went on up the field.

'Keep doing that!' Elie shouted at me.

I kept doing it and Mort kept charging in. It meant I couldn't do much else, but it was working, and we set up two good positions down the right-hand side. The first time Elie played the ball over and Shotty nodded it just wide, and the second time I turned after the tackle and went on into the space where Mort should have been, if he hadn't been flat out on the grass. I got the ball and turned it across and Dicey came out and made a good save at Shotty's feet.

It would have been a better save if he had come out sooner, but I think he wanted everyone to see how brave he was, going down at the forward's feet.

'You watch it, son,' Mort muttered to me.

Even with ten men, there was only one team playing football. The Dixon players were all good on the ball, and they kept funnelling back and drawing Coldwater on to them, and then making quick breaks. It was difficult with our team a man short, and Coldwater having their First-team players, but the real problem was the ref. Almost any time the Dixon players went into tackle, there was a free kick.

By this time Harry, the Dixon Sports Manager, was bouncing up and down on the line and yelling at the ref. We had three players upended, one after the other, and every time Boxer waved play on without even reaching for his whistle.

'Keep playing your football, never mind Boxer Lewis!' Harry shouted, but we couldn't help minding. It wasn't Harry who was being kicked.

Then Elie won the ball on the edge of our area, and he played an angled ball to me. I'd come wide to receive it and Mort was rushing up behind me. Elie was screaming for the play-back and I knew Mort was expecting it, so I shaped for it, and then I dummied, and let the ball run past me, just as Mort went blundering on to what he thought was going to be the lay-off to Elie . . . but the ball wasn't there.

I was clear, on the half-way line, with the Number 5 coming across to cover me, leaving Shotty unmarked.

I got the ball, controlled it, drew the Number 5 on to me, and then I played it straight through the middle to Shotty.

WHAM!

Dicey went full length down by the far post and I think he might have saved it, but he tried to turn what would have been a good save into a brilliant one by holding on to the ball instead of turning it away safely for a corner. The ball flicked off his gloves, nicked against the post, and cannoned into the back of the net.

GOAL! GOAL! GOAL!

Then . . .

C-R-U-M-P!

I felt a tremendous thump. Mort had come hard into me, from behind, with the ball already in the back of the net.

I didn't see the next bit.

I remember lying on the ground, and looking up. There was a whole scrum of players in the middle of the field and Shotty and Mort were rolling over on top of each other. There were fists flying and Boxer was blowing his whistle like mad. He sent Shotty off.

Our goalie came rushing up the field out of his goal, shouting at Boxer about me being thumped, and Harry came on the field yelling and the next moment the whistle was going again and Boxer sent our goalie off as well.

The goalie stood there with his mouth open. He couldn't believe it.

Then Gus shouted, 'One off, all off!' And that is what happened. Our team walked off. Well, the ones who could, did. Our Number 8 was bleeding from a bash one of the Coldwater players had given him, and I couldn't really walk with the pain in my ribs, so Elie and Harry had to help me off while Gus looked after the Number 8.

It was the worst football match I have ever played in. Not *really* a football match at all, because Coldwater Reserves hadn't turned up meaning to play football. They had stuffed their team with big over-age players and gone out to get their revenge for losing to Dixon in the Cup, and they didn't mean to do that by kicking the ball. It was the Dixon Sports' players they were after.

'You all right, son?' Harry asked me.

I was lying on the ground, just beside the minibus, with a big pain in my chest.

'No,' I said.

Harry had some kind of rub, and he put it on my ribs and he sponged my face. There were stud marks right down my side. I don't know when those got there. It must have been one of Mort's studs-up slide-tackles.

'You did really well, son,' Elie said to me.

Boxer Lewis was standing with his lot and started shouting at Harry.

'I'm going to give him a piece of my mind!' Harry said, and he went running up to Boxer.

I thought they were going to fight, but they didn't.

44

I didn't hear what they said.

I didn't care.

I didn't want to know.

I'd come to play football and it wasn't football. It was just a one-sided gang-fight about nothing.

'Is it always like this, this league?' I asked Elie.

He shook his head. 'No,' he said. 'Just them. They are like that, Coldwater. There's always trouble.'

Then somebody said, 'Napper. I told you what would happen!' It was Daniel Rooney. He'd turned up after all, but he'd been sensible and left his boots at home.

'Good goal you got, Napper,' he said. 'The ref needed specs!'

'All you need is to grow a bit, Napper,' Elie said. 'Till then, find a team more your own age to play for, where you won't get picked on.'

'He's right!' said Daniel.

I'd been hoping Dixon might sign me, because they were a proper team and could play a bit, and now they knew I could too, but nobody said anything.

'Have a word with Harry,' Elie said. 'Harry knows a few managers. He might be able to fix you up with somebody.' So I thought I would talk to Harry, but I didn't get the chance.

He'd gone off down to the Common's hut,

having a row about the pitch. Coldwater Reserves had been supposed to get it on one of their pitch permits but now they were refusing to have the permit stamped because they said Dixon had walked off. It was something like that anyway.

My clothes were in the Coldwater dressing-room, down at the sheds.

'We'll go down with you,' Big Shotty the striker offered, but Gus said we would only be asking for trouble, and I'd better hang about until Coldwater had cleared off home.

So I did.

When Daniel and I went down to the dressing-room, we found the Coldwater players had chucked my clothes in the bin at the back.

'Still, you won,' Daniel said.

'Yeah,' I said. 'But who wants a fight like that? I came to play football!'

'Y-e-s,' Daniel said.

I thought a bit. 'Maybe I caused the trouble,' I said. 'The Dixon players kept out of bother when they were being kicked, but when I got kicked they felt they had to do something because I was smaller than everybody else.'

'We'll find a team to play with who are our own age, Napper,' Daniel said.

'Yes,' I said. 'Brilliant!'

Only I had no idea what team it would be, and neither had Daniel. *Not* getting on to the Coldwater Reserves Team was probably just about the best thing that happened to my football career, but I didn't realize it then.

They were a bad team, and I might have got on because I can play, but if I had, I'd have been mixed up in a lot of matches where they went out to kick people, and I'd have learnt nothing.

I limped off home, feeling rotten, thinking things were so bad they could only get better.

Then . . . they got *worse*!

4. Bad Day – Good News

Monday was bad.

Mr Hope saw me in the corridor at break, limping along. My ribs were bruised and battered and my leg had gone stiff as well, which must have been the result of old Mort's crash-tackles.

'Football?' Mr Hope said, stopping in front of me. 'Or was there a war that I missed?'

'Football,' I said.

'Looks like you had some tough opposition,' he said.

I think he was feeling guilty because he was too lazy to get up on Saturday mornings from his nice warm bed.

My sister Avril spent most of Monday going round our school asking if anyone knew of a Nice Well-Organized Baby Football Team run by Somebody's Granny who would look after her Cry-Baby Brother very carefully, because his Mummy didn't want him to be hurt playing with Big Rough Boys. Things like that. She was calling me names and her friend Ugly Irma Bankworth was doing it too. They kept it up all through break, and they were at it again in the playground at dinner-break, when we were kicking in. I had to go in goal because I couldn't run properly and Helena and Daniel and little Jonathan Ramsay were kicking in.

'Don't kick too hard in case you hurt the Baby-Goalie, Helena,' Ugly Irma shouted. 'His Mummy will be cross and his Da-Da will come and scold you.'

'Baby-baby-baby!' Avril chanted.

'Shut up, Avril,' Daniel Rooney said.

'My Baby Brother is not allowed to play with Big Rough Boys like you, Daniel Rooney,' Avril said. 'He might fall on his bottom and cry!'

I was mad.

Daniel shot and I caught the ball and then I booted it straight at Ugly Irma. It whizzed over Irma and . . .

S-M-A-S-H!

The P7 window.

'Ha-ha-ha!' Ugly Irma shouted. 'Who is for it now?'

'You shut up, Irma Bankworth!' Helena Bellow said, running up to her. 'You caused it.'

'Oh-oh-oooh!' Irma shouted. 'Lovey-dovey!'

Then Mr Hope came running out of the staff-room into the playground. He wasn't fair! I didn't mean to bust his rotten window and it wasn't my fault our Science Project was on the other side and the ball bust the spider jar and

49

there were spiders all over the floor. He said the school had no money for fixing windows and replacing valuable equipment and what kind of a young vandal did I think I was and what was I going to do if I went through life losing my temper with people and trying to hurt them instead of learning to sort problems out by talking them over like a reasonable person?

Avril isn't a reasonable person. She is my sister. Ugly Irma isn't my sister, but she isn't reasonable either.

Daniel and Helena Bellow tried telling Mr Hope that it wasn't my fault but he wouldn't listen. He had gone bananas.

That was bad, but it wasn't the worst bit.

When we were back in P7 having a spider hunt to get the spiders back in a new jar, Ugly Irma kept on making jokes and then when we had the spiders jarred she started writing notes, and passing them round.

Notes like:

BIG
BELLOW DRAWERS
LOVES
BABY McCANN

That is how the notes started.

People kept adding bits.

By the time Miss Fellows spotted what was happening and took one of the notes from Stephanie Clark, it looked like this:

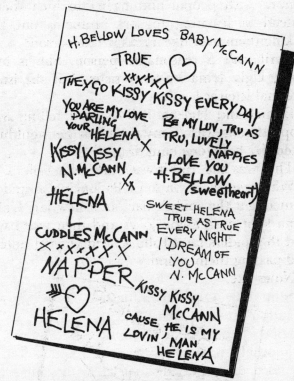

'Well, well, well,' said Miss Fellows.

She smiled as though she thought it was funny and then she tried to pretend she hadn't been smiling and she screwed the note up and put it in the pocket of her dress and went on with the lesson.

'She'll tell all the other teachers!' Avril whispered to me. The trouble was, I thought she was right, and so did Helena. Helena was angry with me, and I had nothing to do with it, so that wasn't fair either.

'I don't care who started it,' Helena said. She had gone tomato red. 'I'm never ever speaking to you again after today, Napper McCann, and I hope your sore leg drops off.'

That was it, apart from Avril shouting, 'Hi, Cuddles!' and bursting into her old donkey laugh when I came into the house after school.

'What's that?' my mum said, looking up.

'Nothing,' I said quickly.

'Just *toujours l'amour*!' Avril said, and she started laughing and rolling around on the sofa and making kissy-kissy noises and pursing up her lips.

'Stop that, Avril!' my mum said.

'I didn't start it,' Avril said.

Then I had to tell her about the P7 window.

'Football, again,' Mum said. 'You weren't supposed to be playing football with your sore leg.'

'I only played a bit,' I said.

'Well, for your information, "Cuddles McCann", you are going to have to help pay for that window,' Mum said, and then she wanted to know why I had 'Napper loves Irma Bankworth' written in big letters on my school-bag.

'I didn't think you even liked Irma,' Mum said.

That set Avril off rolling round the sofa again, and there wasn't any way I could talk myself out of it, because no one would listen to me. I don't know who wrote that on my school-bag but I absolutely do not love old Ugly Irma Bankworth, who is the Biggest Bean Head at Red Row School, not counting my sister Avril, who is the Biggest Bean Head Anywhere in the World or Outer Space Ever.

I went up to my room and started on my Get Irma and Avril plan, but I couldn't work up much interest in it.

Football was up the spout and everybody was laughing at me, even Mum, and I wouldn't ever be able to hold up my head again. It was a bad, bad day.

I was getting ready for school the next day when a letter came for my dad. He opened it when he was eating his breakfast.

'Look at this!' he said, and showed it to my mum.

'Well, I never did!' she gasped. 'That's marvellous!'

'You had better look at this, Napper,' Dad said. 'It ought to cheer you up!'

WARNE COUNTY FOOTBALL CLUB
Est. 1907

General Manager: Owen Lane Stadium
G. Trotman   Owen Lane
                      Warne

To: Mr Donald McCann Esq.

Dear Mr McCann

WARNE COUNTY COMMUNITY
INVOLVEMENT SCHEME

You are no doubt aware from the local press that this Club, in association with the Brontley Building Society and the Burnswicke Community Association is engaged in field-work to encourage the growth of Association Football in the Burnswicke area.

It is our intention to form a junior football squad, which will compete in a competition sponsored by the Brontley Building Society.

I am pleased to inform you that the name of your son, Bernard McCann, has been recommended to us as a player who might benefit from participation in the scheme. I would be grateful if you, as Bernard's parent, or some other person nominated by you to act on your behalf, would attend, with your son, Bernard, an initial trial match at Owen Lane Stadium at 10.30 a.m. this Saturday. I must emphasize that this letter does not imply that Bernard will definitely be amongst those selected for inclusion in the Squad. Final selection will depend on his performance.

It will be necessary for Bernard to bring his own shirt, socks, shorts and boots. Training bibs will be provided by the club. I look forward to meeting you or your representative and Bernard at Owen Lane on Saturday.

Yours sincerely

G. Trotman

G. Trotman
Manager

PS If for any reason Bernard is unable to attend, please contact my office as soon as possible when an alternative date may be arranged.

'WHEEEEEEEEE!' I shouted, and I danced Mum around the room.

A *real* football club, offering me a trial!

Even my dad was impressed!

So was everybody else, when I showed them my letter in school.

Daniel: 'Ea-ay-adioooooooo!'

Mr Hope: 'Well done, Napper, but don't let it interfere with your school work. There are some things in this life even more important than football, you know.' (I think he meant being able to lie in on a Saturday morning and not go off with our team to matches.)

Avril: 'No time for kissy-kissy with Bellow-Drawers if you are going to be a real footballer.'

Miss Fellows: 'I always knew you had it in you, Napper.'

Douglas King: 'Can I have your autograph now, before you are famous?'

P. Scott: 'How come you got a trial, and none of us did?'

Dribbler Wilson: 'Wish it was me!'

Marky Bellow: 'Who cares about football anyway? It's kid's stuff.'

Helena Bellow: 'I'm really really pleased for you, Napper.'

Ugly Irma: 'She would be, wouldn't she?'

Daniel (again): 'How can you go for a trial if your leg is hurt, Napper?'

56

That was worrying me, too.

At first I thought Mum would get Dad to ring G. Trotman, the manager of Warne County, and tell him I was hurt and couldn't play on Saturday. Mum said to wait and see. I did and the leg started getting better straight away. Mum said it was the excitement of being picked but I don't care what it was, the leg just seemed to be better, suddenly.

I wasn't going to let an old injury stop me going for a trial for Warne County, a real semi-pro team, in their stadium at Owen Lane, the same stadium where I scored a hat trick when we played in the final for the Dr Murray Cup.

'It is my lucky ground,' I told Daniel.

I thought if I could get taken on by the Warne County Junior Squad and play in their tournament, I might have a chance to get on for the proper Warne County in a year or two. I would be the youngest player to appear for them and we would have the best non-league run ever in the FA Cup and I would play in the Sixth Round and get a hat trick and Man. United or Liverpool or somewhere would spot me and I would be signed for millions or trillions of pounds.

'Then you can marry Bellow-Drawers and live happily ever after!' Avril said, but I didn't listen to her.

The point was that if I got in their squad I

would be starting out on the way to being Maradona or G. Best or Pelé or somebody else like that on TV.

All the big players had to start somewhere with a small team. I thought there would be training and practice matches with G. Trotman showing us all the things his proper team did.

I spent all week with Daniel and Douglas and Jonathan and Helena practising and I had two training runs on Thursday and Friday to make sure I was fit after my injuries.

Mum got me new shorts and socks and Mr Hope said I could wear my World Famous Number 9 Red Row Stars shirt for the game, provided I brought it back first thing Monday, washed.

Then Saturday came, and the Trial Match!

5. Warne County Colts: Squad Trial

Reds v. Blues
Referee: T. Cowans (ex-Scotland!)
Venue: Owen Lane Stadium, Warne
In Attendance: G. Trotman, Manager,
Warne County
D. W. Ledley, Coach

G. Trotman, who used to play for Oldham, had us all together in the main dressing-room under the stand at Owen Lane.

He had a track suit with WARNE COUNTY on the front, which is the one he uses when he is coaching the big team and in the dug-out at matches.

He introduced D. W. Ledley, who was to coach the squad, and T. Cowans. He said T. Cowans was famous and used to play for Scotland. I don't know if he was joking. D. W. Ledley seemed to think it was funny, and they were both laughing.

G. Trotman didn't seem to think it was funny.

He started being very serious. We all had to sit down on the benches round the dressing-room and the ones there wasn't room for had to stand.

Then he gave us a speech, from a bit of paper in his hand.

The first bit was all about Warne County being a family club and part of the community, and it was the same sort of thing he'd said to all the grown-ups in the Club Room before he brought us down to the dressing-room.

Then he said, 'OK, lads. That's the guff that's going in the paper. You can all read it, next Thursday, with your grannies and aunties. Now I'm going to give you the bottom line.'

T. Cowans, who may have played for Scotland only we weren't sure if it was a joke, said something, and G. Trotman glared at him.

'Sorry, boss,' T. Cowans said.

'You want to be footballers,' G. Trotman said. 'That is why you are here. Some of you may make it, but most of you won't. That's straight. If we get two or three of you who make the grade, that's more than we can reasonably expect. So a lot of you are going to be disappointed. Right?'

Nobody said anything. We all sat there and shuffled.

'You want to be footballers,' G. Trotman

repeated, 'OK, here's your chance. There are forty of you here today . . .'

'Forty-seven, boss,' T. Cowans put in.

'Yes, forty-seven,' G. Trotman said. 'Every time I look round there's another one! Some of you we are seeing for the first time, some played in last week's run-out. You are here for a trial game, which will give you a chance to show us what you can do. We're going to split you into two groups, Reds versus Blues. You'll all get on, some time during the game, maybe only for twenty minutes or so. This isn't a match, it's a trial. It lasts as long as we need it to last, which is long enough for Davie and myself and Mr Cowans to see what you can do. At the end, we'll be knocking about half of you off the list. That's tough, but that is the way it is. It doesn't mean you are finished. It means that we have to leave somebody out. We have two weeks to get this up and running before we play Tommy Cowans's Big Testimonial Match. The Youth Squad game will go on directly before that, under floodlights, so that our sponsors get the maximum publicity for their money. We have two weeks to build a team – a team that can do a job for this club. That doesn't give us time to mess about. It is serious!'

'Like deadly serious!' said T. Cowans, with a grin.

G. Trotman turned to him and frowned. 'Wrap it up, Tommy!' he said.

Then he went on with his speech. 'Today isn't a game, it's a sort-out. If you get past this one, you'll be invited back, and then we'll take a look at you in real match conditions. Any questions?'

Nobody said anything.

'Right!' Mr Trotman said. 'Get stripped.'

Nobody talked to anybody, we were all too nervous.

I thought that there would be a lot of players that I would know, because of playing for Red Row, but there weren't and I didn't know why. The only one I saw was Joe Fish, the St Gabriel's centre-half. Looking round, I could see I wasn't the youngest, but I was nearly the youngest. They all seemed to be B-I-G. I thought that didn't matter because we had all filled in forms giving our ages and they would see I had potential. I thought they would prefer young players because they would be building for the future. I was hoping they would, anyway.

Mr D. W. Ledley read our names off a list and Joe and I were both on the Blues, which meant we got blue bibs with numbers on. There were twenty-two bibs of each colour, so some people didn't have one, but they were told they would get one later when somebody came off. I was Number 15 on the Blues, so I thought that I wouldn't get on to begin with, but that I would get on later.

I put the bib on over my famous Red Row Number 9. Mr Hope had said I could wear it because it is the shirt I wore when I scored a hat trick the last time I played at my lucky ground. I thought it might have been in that game that I was spotted for a trial, because G. Trotman might have been there. It didn't really matter how I'd been recommended to County anyway. The important thing was being there, and playing well. Then we went out.

'One to 11, both teams, on the pitch, the rest of you sit down,' D. W. Ledley said.

It turned out that 1 to 11 on the Blues team included two goalies, a big one called Markham whom D. W. Ledley seemed to know, and another called McKee whom he didn't. McKee got in the team and Markham came off, and Number 12 went on, which meant there were two more to go on the Blues before they came to me.

'What about positions?' Joe Fish asked. He'd come to sit on the bench along the touch-line with me, because we knew each other, and we didn't know anybody else. 'They're just putting people anywhere!'

We thought it was stupid.

The forms we'd filled in were just age and address and name of Parent or Guardian and their signature, stuff like that. They didn't say anything about what positions we played, and D. W. Ledley didn't seem to be worried about it either.

He got the Blue team around him and stuck people in positions.

G. Trotman was doing the same with the Reds.

Then T. Cowans came running out of the tunnel on to the pitch and he went to the centre circle and blew his whistle and everybody lined up.

Pssst! T. Cowans blew his whistle and we started. D. W. Ledley was on one side of the pitch, down the touch-line, with a clipboard and pen, and G. Trotman was on the other.

The players were all good.

There were people doing tricky things on the ball all over the pitch and yelling and making runs and doing flick passes and hard tackles. It was a kind of show-off game, rather than a football match.

They were all going about ten million miles an hour.

Then G. Trotman waved at T. Cowans and T. Cowans blew his whistle and G. Trotman came on and read everybody a lecture in the centre circle, and after that people started passing the ball a bit.

It got more like real football.

I was watching the strikers, because I am a striker.

The first two weren't great, although there was one of them who got a goal when the goalie called McKee missed the ball and gave him a clear header. He went mad, jumping about, and I suppose he was right because he knew he would be kept on for the next trial. Anybody who got a goal would be. That's what I thought, anyway.

McKee looked sick.

He got really nervous and he missed the next shot completely, but it hit the post and came out. Then the Red Number 9 bashed the ball wide of the post with an open goal in front of him, so that was one striker I didn't have to worry about.

D. W. Ledley went down behind the goal and said something to McKee, but the goalie didn't get anything else to do until he was substituted and Markham went on.

D. W. Ledley came up to the bench and he said, 'Right! 13 to 17 on!'

That meant me, N. McCann Super Star!

'Where do I go?' I asked him.

'Right-back,' he said.

'I'm a striker,' I said.

He grinned at me.

'Listen, son, everybody's a striker. You go right-back.'

So I went right-back.

Joe was put up front, but he isn't a striker. We both looked at each other.

'Swopsy?' Joe said.

'G-r-e-a-t!' I said.

The second time the ball went into touch I moved up a bit and Joe dropped back. We were nearly in our usual positions and we thought that would give us a chance to show what we could do and then we could get in the team.

Then I got the ball.

I was in my own half and their Number 14 came across and I showed him the ball, enough to commit him to the tackle. Then I switched it inside and belted forward. I was heading for goal and their Number 11 came across and tried to side-swipe me. I jinked over him and then I got a look at goal. I could see the goalie coming out and I chipped the ball towards his back post, thinking I would score another N. McCann Super Goal with almost my first touch of the ball. Then I would be sure of getting into the proper match, where they were going to pick the Squad.

It went wrong.

It wasn't an N. McCann Super Goal.

It wasn't even anything looking like a goal. The ball kind of bobbed as I went to hit it and my chip shot turned into a slice and went off towards the sideline. The Blues winger went after it but even he couldn't catch it. It went out about level with the far side of the penalty area.

'Optimistic, kid!' T. Cowans said, running past me up the field. 'Neat, if it had worked!'

I had been about ten metres out of the area, with the goalie just leaving his box to meet me. If the ball hadn't bounced so badly it would have been a great chip over his head and an almost certain goal. But the ball did bounce and I was left looking silly.

I went back downfield.

They'd seen I could beat people, anyway, even good players, who were bigger than me. I reckoned I could do it again and I would take them on and waltz through the defence and then maybe, instead of shooting, so they wouldn't think I was goal-greedy I would slip the ball inside and somebody else would lash in a great shot. The goalie would save it and I would touch away the rebound and they would say I had made it and scored it too, because I have an eye for the half-chance.

'You!' D. W. Ledley shouted from the line.

I didn't know who he was shouting at.

I thought it was somebody else.

'15!'

It wasn't somebody else, it was me.

I turned round.

It was the wrong moment to do it, because just as I turned to look at him our Number 10 played the ball to where I should have been running and I wasn't.

'Keep your eye on the ball, son!' D. W. Ledley yelled. I ran up to tackle the boy in possession, but he switched it inside and the boy he switched it to played it back. I was left trailing after him and looking daft because I shouldn't have run at him, I should have funnelled back. Our Number 3, a boy called Purdy, came across and cut the ball off.

'You!' D. W. Ledley was shouting at me again.

'What position do you call that? Right-back.' Right-BACK!'

So I had to go right-back.

'14, UP!' D. W. Ledley yelled and Joe had to move forward.

I was fed up! I'd mucked up the one chance I'd got and missed by a mile when I could have passed inside, and now I was in trouble for not being in position, when right-back isn't my position to begin with.

D. W. Ledley would think I didn't know one position from another and I was greedy on the ball, trying to show off by beating people and scoring long-range goals.

Joe was in trouble too. He is all right when people are coming at him, but he was playing where I should have been, going forward alongside the big Number 11, who was called Matty, and Joe isn't good at that. He always looked good when it was one of the school matches, Red Row against St Gabriel's, because half the kids on both teams were small ones or couldn't play much. The Trial Match was different, because everyone could play, and Joe looked bad.

He tried to move forward, but he got his runs wrong. He was offside, the first time, in a position that no one who is used to going up front would be, and the second time he got on to the end of a ball that Matty switched back to him but he didn't know what to do with it. Before he could play it the back came in and hammered him.

'Slow!' D. W. Ledley bawled at him. 'Wake up, son!'

Matty shouted at Joe too, standing there with his hands on his hips. He was getting at Joe for not feeding it through to him, when he'd got clear of the Red's midfield.

Then they changed the teams round again, and I thought I would get going forward but they didn't change me. They put me in the middle of the defence, which was stupid, because they'd brought on a big kid called Lorenzo for the Reds. I was supposed to mark him and he was about twice my size.

He had me running all over the place! I didn't know whether to hold my position in the centre or go after him. The first time he went I didn't go. The kid called Ronnie Purdy who was playing alongside me yelled at me and our keeper had to come out and make a big diving save at Lorenzo's feet.

The next time he went it was out to the left, which is my weak side, but I went after him. He showed me the ball, and then he booted it hard and steamed past. He was too fast for me and I couldn't get back at him and he shot.

Our new goalie was a kid called Ally. He'd made the save at Lorenzo's feet and this time he did another super one, getting up in the air and parrying the ball back. Lorenzo was sprinting in to score but Purdy managed to get to the ball first and turn it round for a corner. Lorenzo said something to the goalie and glared at me and then, when the corner came across, he went in past me like a flash and BANG!

Goal.

Lorenzo was on his knees in the net clutching the ball and the goalie was yelling at me for not cutting him out. I yelled back at him for not coming out and he yelled that I should have had it covered.

'You want to grow a bit, son,' T. Cowans said to me, when they were going back up the field. 'Either that, or be first.'

He was right and I knew he was.

This is what happened:

This is what *should* have happened:

Lorenzo had come in from behind me, so I couldn't spot his run. When the ball came, he was across me, blocking me, and he had a free header.

My being smaller than Lorenzo wouldn't have mattered if I'd moved more sharply to the ball as it came. Then I would have been across him, and he couldn't have played the ball without fouling me. I hadn't done it.

I tried backing off him but he was still too fast. Then I thought I would use his speed, making him run where I wanted him to go. Twice it worked well, and he ran into our defence. Purdy yelled at me and clapped encouragingly. The third time he got clear of everybody and came at me again, head on, like a bull. I knew he was going to boot the ball and outrun me. It was one on one, bearing down on the left side of the penalty area. Joe Fish had seen I was in trouble, and he was pounding back, but losing ground. I thought the only thing I could do was to turn Lorenzo so that he would go outside me, which might let Joe get close enough to get his tackle in. This is what I did:

I turned right shoulder on to him, a half-turn, and he saw the movement, and booted the ball for the space I'd left him. It meant that as he moved wide he lost control and momentum. If he had thought about what he was doing, he would have tried to go inside me, bearing directly down on goal, but he didn't. He saw the open space I was offering him, and bulldozed into it, head down, rushing after the ball with the idea that his size and speed would carry him out of the problem he was running into. The switch gave Joe just the chance he needed to gain a metre or two, enough to get in his tackle.

Joe crashed into him, but the tackle was late. PENALTY!

I'd made Lorenzo switch direction, putting him across the line of Joe's run and pushing him away from goal at the same time. Joe had read what I was doing, and gone in to nick the ball away for a corner, but he had missed.

'Blast,' Joe said. There was no doubt about it. He had been late and almost from behind, and T. Cowans, the ref, couldn't have given anything else.

'You watch it, son!' Lorenzo said to Joe, and then he picked himself up and ran to the ball to make sure he would get to take the kick.

I thought our goalie might save it, because he'd made two great saves already, but he didn't. The penalty wasn't well taken, and the goalie might have got it, but he had guessed the wrong way. He stuck out a hand and got a touch, but the ball was buried in the net.

Lorenzo went, 'Yup! Yup! Yup!' punching the air in triumph, and then he did a cart-wheel!

Two goals, and he'd only been on ten minutes!

He knew he was in the squad.

I knew I was out of it.

I was too.

They switched the teams again, after the goal, and I had to give my bib to a guy called Zico Ryan, who used to play in our school games. He'd grown a bit, so I hadn't recognized him. He was a striker too, and they put him down the middle for my team, the Blues.

I didn't wait to see what he would do. I knew Zico could play a bit and I'd seen Matty, the big one who started off for the Blues. Lorenzo had got two goals and there were still piles of players on the line.

Probably they were strikers too, mostly, because everybody wants to be a striker.

I went to the dressing-room with Joe Fish and the goalie, Ally.

Ally was looking chuffed.

'You're in,' Joe told him. 'You had a real good game.'

'Should have got the penalty,' Ally said. 'I thought he would place it and he just blasted it.'

I think goalies are lucky. Nobody blames them for not stopping penalties. Ally might have stopped it if he had stood his ground, but he would have looked foolish if Lorenzo had placed the shot.

'Wasn't even well hit!' Ally said.

'I gave it away,' Joe said, miserably.

'You might be all right,' I told Joe. 'They could see you were covering me, because I couldn't manage Lorenzo.'

'Trying to play the ball, wasn't I?' Joe said.

'Yeah,' I said.

'Still a penalty though,' Ally said. 'You were

coming in late and from behind. That's always iffy.'

'Well, he was quicker on the ball than I thought he'd be,' Joe said. 'I didn't mean to bring him down. He'd lost it, then he went over my leg.'

It wasn't any good talking about it.

Joe and I went up to the stand, where Dad was sitting with Daniel and Joe Fish's auntie, Mrs Ruby Squirrel, who'd come because his dad works Saturdays and his mum is in hospital.

'Well done, boys,' she said.

'Good on you,' my dad said.

Daniel didn't say anything.

My dad and Mrs Squirrel went back to talking about how Mrs Fish's bad foot was. They didn't know anything about football. I suppose they thought we'd done well just being out there.

'Well, you got this far, anyway,' Daniel said to me.

I felt really cheated!

It was supposed to be a proper football club and they deliberately played us out of position even when we'd told them.

The trial went on, and on and on. I didn't watch it much. I didn't want to, because I knew I wasn't going to be in the team.

'Cheer up, Napper,' Joe's auntie said to me.

Then we had to go down into the dressing-room again, and Mr Trotman and D. W. Ledley came in with their clipboards and they started reading out the numbers of the players they wanted at the training ground on Wednesday for the Reds versus Blues Final Selection Match.

'Red Bib,' Mr Trotman said. '2, 7, 9, 10, 11, 12, 15, 16, 17, 18, 19, 20, 21, 22.'

That was fourteen red bibs, so it meant that there could only be ten of the blues, which was our team.

'Blue Bibs,' Mr Trotman continued. '4, 5, 6, 7, 8, 15 . . .'

FIFTEEN!

I was IN!

I didn't even hear the other numbers.

Joe wasn't in them. Then he was. Mr Trotman said, 'Subs,' and he called 14, which was Joe's number.

'Sorry, the rest of you,' Mr Trotman added. 'Don't let it get to you! Maybe you'll make it some other day.'

Then Lorenzo came out of the crowd. He looked really wild. He went right up to Mr Trotman.

'Mister, I got two goals!' he said.

'Yes. Sorry, son,' Mr Trotman said.

'Two goals . . . that's what it's all about!' Lorenzo was nearly crying. He had his fists clenched, and he was shouting at Mr Trotman.

At least it started out as a shout, and then his voice kind of broke.

'I gotta be in the squad if I got two goals!' he said.

'Learn when to part with the ball, son,' Mr Trotman said. 'All you do is put your head down and run.'

'I STUCK IT IN, twice!' Lorenzo yelled at him.

'Sorry, son,' Mr Trotman said, and he patted Lorenzo on the shoulder, and then he went out.

D. W. Ledley went over to Lorenzo and he started to say something to him, but Lorenzo wasn't having any. He started calling Warne County and Mr Trotman and D. W. Ledley and everybody who'd been playing a lot of names, and then he grabbed up his bag and ran out of the dressing-room. Mr Trotman and Mr D. W. Ledley had a talk with the mums and dads and guardians of the players who were in the squad and then we all went home. My dad and Daniel were delighted! We spent ages talking about it in the car going home.

'I don't understand how they did the picking,' I said, and I told them about Lorenzo with his two goals not being in the squad.

'Oh,' my dad said. 'You mean the big boy who scored the goals? He doesn't know anything about football.'

I didn't know what to make of that. My dad doesn't know anything about football either.

He never played because he had some illness when he was little and couldn't run much.

'He *looked* good,' my dad said. 'But that was only because he was bigger than anybody else. The rest of you will catch up on him when you grow a bit, and then where will he be?'

'Yes,' I said. 'But . . . two goals!'

'You didn't get any and you are in the team,' Daniel said. 'I don't understand it.'

'I didn't do anything much. I didn't get a chance to,' I said.

'Yes you did,' my dad said. 'Even I could see that. When you had the ball, you tried to use it, and when you were marking that big boy you realized he was too fast for you, and you tried to find a way to cope with the problems he was giving you. I expect that impressed them a lot.' I thought it might have impressed them more if I had succeeded, instead of letting Lorenzo score two goals.

Perhaps G. Trotman the manager and D. W. Ledley and T. Cowans had deliberately played some of us out of position, so they could see if we could think. I told Daniel that was it anyway.

'If you can play football you can play anywhere,' I said.

'I don't think that is right,' Daniel said. 'I'm a striker. I wouldn't want to play libero.'

'If you're a striker, you'll have to play against

teams who play with a libero,' I said. 'You ought to know how to play it, and then adapt your own game to fit the position if you find you have to play there. A good player out of position will still be a good player, but a bad player will just look silly, like Lorenzo.'

'And score two goals!' Daniel said, sounding unconvinced.

I thought about that.

Big stupid footballers like Lorenzo would never get any better, but the smaller players who could read the game and adapt to what was happening might.

The important thing for me to do in the Selection Trial was to let them see that I could work out what was happening on the field . . . like working out that Lorenzo was too fast for me . . . and then think my way round the problem. That way I might get into the team!

Or I might end up out of it, like Lorenzo!

The best thing would still be to do the thing I do best, and start scoring some Napper Super Goals!

6. The Big Row

It was really brilliant.

When I got to school on Monday morning everybody had heard that I'd been picked for the Final Trial. They all came up to me in the playground and congratulated me, even Ugly Irma. They thought I was going to be the Greatest Footballer Ever out of Red Row and I would be famous and go on TV and have my name in the papers and everything.

It was the best ever.

Then it all went wrong.

There was a big row and I thought I wasn't going to make it to the Final Trial.

My dad had given me a note saying he would be grateful if Mr Hope would allow Bernard to leave school at half-past twelve on Wednesday in order to take part in the Final Selection Trial for Warne County Colts Football Team.

I thought it would be all right because Mr Hope would be pleased with somebody from a small school like ours getting through to the Final Trial.

Then Mr Hope sent Dribbler Wilson down to the P7 Room and said he wanted to see me in his office, so down I went.

'Well, Napper,' he said. 'I gather you made it! Good boy!'

'Yes, sir,' I said.

'Congratulations!' he said. 'One up for Red Row on St Gabriel's!'

'Joe Fish made it too,' I said. 'We are both in the Final Trial.'

'Joe isn't at St Gabriel's,' Mr Hope said. 'He's moved on.'

'Right,' I said.

'Quite a distinction for the school,' he said. 'So all our work with the football team last year hasn't been wasted. Yes! Yes!'

I'd begun to worry in case he wasn't going to let me go or something, but now I wasn't worried, because he was so pleased. I told him about the Final Trial. It was to be called Warne County Colts 'A' v. Warne County Colts 'B' and it would be a kind of Probables v. Possibles. I didn't know whether I was a Probable or a Possible because they hadn't told us yet, but if I got in the Final 18-man Squad, then I would have a chance of playing in the team's first-ever real match against Boyne Dynamo Youth Squad on the night of the T. Cowans Testimonial Match.

'Tommy Cowans?' he said, very impressed. 'He used to play for Scotland.'

'And there are lots of real players playing and we'll have our match before them and there'll be a proper crowd and everything and it'll be floodlit!' I said.

'*If* you make a go of it in this Final Trial,' he said. 'Am I right?'

'Right,' I said.

'Yes, well . . .' he said. 'That is a bit of a problem. Twelve thirty.'

He sat there, looking at Dad's letter.

'I have to get off at twelve thirty because I have to get over to the ground to get the coach and it is a two o'clock kick-off at Back End, which is where we are playing. The match can't kick off later because they haven't any floodlights,' I said. 'It is just a training ground.'

'You want the whole afternoon off to play football?' he said.

'But . . .'

'And this won't be the end of it, will it?' he asked. 'So much for the Football Club and Community Relations! I have a school to run, in common with a number of head teachers whose boys will be involved. What are we supposed to do if we have pupils coming in every other week wanting time off for this Community Relations exercise the football club is putting on? Education comes first, Napper.'

'It won't be every other week, sir,' I said. 'Just this one. There's only *one* trial, then it will

83

be matches, and matches will be Saturday mornings, so they won't interfere with school.'

'I'd need to be sure about that,' he said.

I mumbled something.

He must have known what I was thinking
... I'd miss the Final Trial because he was
mean about one old mouldy school afternoon
and maybe I would never get another chance.

'I'll have to speak to some of the other head
teachers, Napper,' he said. 'Sorry, but this thing
has implications you don't grasp. If we all say
the same thing, maybe we can make your precious football club realize that they are dealing
with *school* children, not adult players who are
at their beck and call. I don't mind co-operating
with outside-school activities, but they have got
to be outside school hours, and this thing is just
beginning. If we let it ride now, it is going to
begin the *wrong* way round, with the football
club dictating to the schools when we can have
our pupils.'

'But . . .'

'You aren't the only one, Napper,' he said.
'I've had four head teachers on to me this
morning already, all with the same problem.
We have to take a stand!'

'Does that mean you won't let me go?' I said.

'It means I don't know,' he said. 'I need to
think about it, and talk it over with the other
head teachers.'

Then he said I could go back to class.

And he said: 'I know this won't seem reasonable to you, Napper, because it looks like just one afternoon off. But if your football team wants our co-operation the organizers will have to work for it, not demand it as a right.'

He wasn't going to let me go.

When I went home I thought I would tell my dad and he would go down and see Mr Hope and tell him I had to go because of being a footballer some day and it being my big chance.

I thought at least my dad would see it my way.

'Well,' he said. 'I don't know.'

Then he said it would be better if we let the Football Club sort it out with the schools and it would probably be all right in the end, because if all the Heads said 'no', then there couldn't *be* a Final Trial, and they would have to think again at the Football Club.

'If there isn't a trial, we might not have a team,' I said. 'Mr Trotman might get fed up and scrap the whole thing.'

'Wait and see,' Dad said. 'I don't think that will happen.'

So I had to wait.

'You could have a strike,' Avril said.

'What do you mean?'

'If the teachers don't let you go, you could

have a strike and say you are not going to school,' she said. 'If you all did it . . .'

'We all go to different schools,' I said. 'That's the trouble. If it was only Mr Hope, I think it would be all right, but it isn't. It is all the head teachers, and they think they have to stick together, so he might not be able to let me go even if he wants to.'

I was really surprised at Avril because she doesn't like football and she calls me names and she gangs up on me with Ugly Irma, but this time Avril and Irma seemed to be on my side.

The next day Avril and Irma and Helena Bellow and Daniel Rooney and Dribbler Wilson organized a deputation without telling me and they went to see Mr Hope. He said they were very thoughtful to speak on my behalf like that and he was pleased with them but he couldn't allow it to interfere with his decision. He would have to go along with what all the head teachers agreed.

'So I think you have had it, Napper,' Dribbler said to me.

'Maybe they'll fix a different time,' Daniel said.

Then, just about lunch-time, Miss Fellows came to our room and told me I had to go and see Mr Hope again.

'You're getting everybody into a tizzy with your football, Napper,' she said.

'Yes, miss,' I said. 'It isn't fair.'

'That's a matter of opinion!' she said. 'I don't think your precious Football Club is being very fair to all the schools, do you? We have a job to do too, you know. Educating you lot!'

I didn't think Mr Hope was going to let me go.

But he D-I-D.

'Once only, Napper!' he said. 'We've had to take a tough line with your Football Club and its managers. But you're getting your chance. Make sure you use it!'

I went back to P7 and told them, and everybody cheered.

7. Warne County Colts: Final Trial

WARNE COUNTY COLTS FINAL TRIAL
Warne County Colts 'A' v. Warne County
Colts 'B'
Referee: A. Mallon (Warne County Reserves)
Venue: Back Lane Training Ground
(Warne County FC)
In Attendance: G. Trotman, Manager,
Warne County
D. W. Ledley, Coach, Warne County Colts
T. Cowans (ex-Scotland)

G. Trotman ticked our names off his list as we were getting on the coach at Owen Lane. The coach was to take us out to the Warne County Training Ground at Back End.

'Twenty-five,' he said. 'All present and correct, and raring to go.'

Nobody laughed.

I sat beside Ally, the goalkeeper, on the coach.

Neither of us said anything for a while, and

neither did anybody else. It was the most uncheery coach trip I have ever been on.

'Rotten, isn't it?' Ally said nervously.

'Yeah,' I said, 'only *brilliant* too!'

We were in the Final Trial. If we did well, we might be picked to make the real team, Warne County Colts, and play at Owen Lane against Boyne Dynamo.

D. W. Ledley came down the bus, with a clipboard, talking to each one of us.

'Scott?' he said. 'And McCann?'

We said that was us.

'You'll be starting in the Bs, Scott,' he said to Ally. 'Doesn't mean you are a B. You might switch over to the As second half, or you might be off. We have three keepers, so it is up to you.'

Ally nodded.

D. W. Ledley flicked through his notes.

'Weak on crosses,' he said. 'Five crosses, and you didn't come once. Dodgy!'

Ally squirmed on his seat.

'Still, you didn't know your defenders,' D. W. Ledley added. 'Dangerous business leaving your line if the cover isn't there.'

'Yeah,' Ally said, glad to be let off the hook.

He might be off it, but I was on it. I'd *been* one of his defenders and I don't know a lot about covering cross-balls defensively.

'McCann?' D. W. Ledley said.

'That's me,' I said.

'Poor in the air,' he said. 'Still, you were defending, which put you on the wrong foot, if you are used to being up front. The big lad who beat you could use his strength . . . if nothing else!' He grinned. He meant Lorenzo. It was the only defensive aerial ball that had come my way, and Lorenzo had beaten me to it.

'You'll be on for the Bs, second half, McCann,' he said. 'On the small side for this team, aren't you?'

Then he went off.

'Both Bs,' Ally said glumly. 'That means we're second team, *possibles* and not probables.'

Ally was all right. He was on for the whole match, probably, and he might be put into the As. I was substitute for the Bs, and I'd only get

a half to show them what I could do. I thought it was probably because I was smaller than most of them, but it still didn't seem fair. I'd had about twenty minutes on the field so far, out of position, and now I was sub for the Bs and only going to get a half.

We arrived at the ground and went to the dressing-room and D. W. Ledley read out the team lists:

'A' Team	'B' Team
Bantam	Scott
Brocken	Holton
Purdy	Reid
McCall	Subandric
Bird	Jenks
Mole	Fish
Brown	Wallace
Zan	Chamberlain
Henchley	Jezz
Singh	Matthews
Alexiou	Dole
Sub: Usiskin	Sub: McCann

'McKee?' D. W. Ledley said.

'Yes?'

'You get stripped as well, son. You'll get on one half, at one end or the other ... that depends on the two keepers who are starting.'

McKee didn't look pleased.

I thought he was lucky to be in the match at all, because he'd done *nothing* when he was in goal in the Reds v. Blues, except miss a few.

'I reckon he's somebody's cousin!' Ally said, when we were going out.

The As were playing in Warne County home strip, which is black and white stripes, and the Bs were in the away strip, which is yellow. I had a yellow jersey with number 14 on it. I don't know why it had 14; there didn't seem to be a 12 or 13.

'Good luck,' I said to Joe Fish. They had slotted him in at midfield, which is where Joe likes to go, and D. W. Ledley had talked a lot to him.

I went on the line, with T. Cowans, ex-Scotland.

He started shouting as soon as the game began.

They were all at it, G. Trotman and D. W. Ledley and T. Cowans.

They kept shouting at people about their marking and their passes and what position they were supposed to be in. I felt really out of it.

'Don't worry,' T. Cowans said to me. 'You'll get on soon.'

Matthews, the big striker who'd played up front for the Reds in the First Trial, was making runs all over the place.

'He's a goer!' T. Cowans said, after Matthews had taken one down far out on the right, squirmed past his man, and flighted the ball across goal to the second striker, Jezz. Jezz got up above his man and got a header in, but the 'A' goalie, Tony Bantam, got down at his near post and smothered the ball. Everybody clapped.

Then Matthews got away down the middle, all on his own, and he really blasted it. Another great save. Tony Bantam took the ball at full stretch, in the air, and held on.

'Yo! Yo! Yo!' T. Cowans said. 'There's your keeper, Davie!'

'Reckon so,' D. W. Ledley said.

McKee looked really glum.

Joe Fish was having a hard time of it. I was watching him because I was up for Joe, and at the same time I wanted to see how the other strikers would do.

I'd already seen what Jezz and big Matty – that's what they called Matthews – could do and I thought there would probably only be three strikers in the final squad for the match. I wanted Joe to be all over one of them, which would leave me one less to beat.

Joe was up against a little one, Zan, who was very tricky on the ball. He kept making runs, and jinking, but he didn't link up well with the 'A' team's other strikers, Danny Mole and

Lester Singh. Mole was strong, and better on the ball than Matty, but he kept being caught offside, and the big back, Tom Brocken, who was captain of the As, started yelling at him. Lester Singh was very fast, probably the fastest player on the field, but he did a lot of running into blind alleys, and was shouted at.

Then Danny Mole and Zan were switched, so that Danny was coming through the centre at Joe, and Zan was playing off him. It should have been better for Joe, because Danny Mole was big and clumsy, but he was strong, and he was able to break Joe's tackles.

He got through Joe, on the edge of the area, and he drove in a blinder which Ally got up to but couldn't hold and the ball broke off a little jinky player called Alexiou, who lobbed it back towards the empty net. Joe had covered back, and he came in behind the keeper, with the ball just bouncing on the line, and hooked it clear.

'Well covered, son!' D. W. Ledley shouted, and he ticked something on his clipboard pad.

Joe started coming off Danny, and the next two occasions Danny overran the ball and Joe nicked it from him. I thought he was doing really well, considering how big Danny Mole was. The third time Danny got the ball and turned, Joe turned with him to force him to the right, but Danny just kept on turning. Then he hit a great ball inside the area and Lester caught

it on the instep, took two strides and found Ally
Scott coming off his line to meet him.

GOAL!

Ally was really unlucky. He spread himself
well, and got a hand to the ball, but it bobbed
up and Zan managed to nudge it with his thigh
and the ball went over the line.

Ally got the ball out of the net, looking really
miserable.

Tony Bantam, at the other end, was pulling
off great saves and hanging on to the ball, and
Ally had had two difficult ones and each time
he'd blocked the shot but not been able to
hold it.

'Hard luck,' McKee said, grinning all over
his face.

'Kid did well to get out so fast,' T. Cowans
said, frowning at him. 'Reckon you can do
better?'

McKee just shrugged.

They went to kick off again and then Mole
got away down the right and he was in full
flight when the Bs' back crash-tackled him,
two-footed.

Big blast on the whistle, and a lecture from
the ref, but he wasn't sent off. It was Mole who
had to come off and the As' sub, Usiskin, was
pulling off his track-suit top, but D. W. Ledley
stopped him and called me over.

'Change jerseys, son,' he said. 'You're on!'

So I was on the As, which was the Probables, and not the Bs, which was the Possibles, and I thought that must be better and it was.

I was up front, partnering Zan, the tricky one, with Lester Singh, the speedy one, outside me. I was up against Jenks, not Joe Fish. I didn't want to be on Joe, because he knows my game, and I thought I would have more chance with a player who didn't know me.

First ball . . . I was out on the left, coming off Jenks to draw him out of the middle, and the As' captain, Brocken, had the ball and was coming over the half-way line. He played a clever ball behind Jenks and in my path.

Ally came haring out of goal. I let him come and then I played the ball inside to Alexiou.

This is what I did:

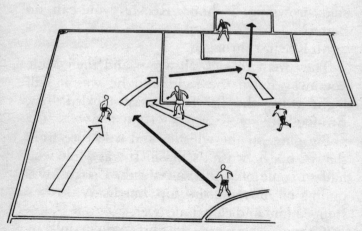

GOAL! GOAL! GOAL!

Goal laid on by Napper McCann, Super Star!

Alexiou only had to walk it in. Ally was left stranded by my through-ball, and he could only watch.

D. W. Ledley started yelling at Jenks, and he tightened up on me. The next time I got the ball he forced me wide, and all I could do was play it back to Tom Brocken, who was steaming up behind me. Brocken got his cross in, and Zan got on to it, but he tried to beat three men twice, and in the end Joe Fish got him. It was a pity because I was clear and Alexiou was unmarked as well. Alexiou was really *good*, he always seemed to have space to move in. That's what I thought anyway. The defender he was up against looked really disgusted.

Then I was clear on another ball from big Brocken, and one-two-ed it with Zan, but Zan delayed his pass, and I was offside on the run-in. I linked up with Alexiou again and he gave me a great ball. I got round Jenks and put in a screamer from the left and Ally got up and held on to it this time. Everybody clapped, except McKee.

Then Ally was taken off and McKee was put on.

Ally looked sick. He thought his chance had gone.

I thought it was great, because I'd seen McKee in the first match and I knew he was slow off his line and his handling was poor and he was only in the trial because he was somebody's cousin.

I got clean through.

WHAM!

Then Lester Singh got three chances and . . .

D. W. Ledley and G. Trotman and T. Cowans were cheering McKee like mad and Lester Singh was looking sick, because he had had three good shots saved one after the other. I didn't get another chance before half-time, so I hadn't done much, but I had laid on one good ball. The Captain, Tom Brocken, came up to me as we were going to the line and said, 'Well played, Titch!' so I was pleased.

G. Trotman and D. W. Ledley and T. Cowans called Brocken over and they had a long talk, and then they started marking their lists.

Then they started rearranging the teams.

'Change jerseys, McCann,' D. W. Ledley said to me, and I was in the B team, out of the Probables.

We lined up. I saw Tom Brocken was in behind me, so he was in the Bs as well and I thought maybe I *wasn't* out, because he seemed to be the best player on the As and he had been organizing everything.

McKee was in the As' goal, and Ally was brought back on for the Bs and Bantam was out, but he was out with a big grin on his face after D. W. Ledley had talked to him. I thought he probably knew he was in, which wasn't surprising because he'd been making good saves right through the first half.

They had changed the teams about so much

that I was a bit muddled up. It didn't make sense to keep switching people. This time I was Bs and I had Tom Brocken and Joe Fish behind me with Alexiou out wide and Matty in front. I was pleased about that because they could all play.

The trouble was that the As went straight into the attack and we didn't get the ball to play with. Zan and Jezz were doing business for them, and three times in the first ten minutes they got clear. The first time Zan beat two men, including Tom Brocken, and he should have scored but Ally came out and cut him off. Then Jezz got through and did a one-two, but the pass was late from Zan and Jezz was offside. Then Jezz did another run that had everybody clapping, but he miscued his pass and the ball went round the post.

'He can play a bit, that Zan,' Alexiou said to me, looking anxious.

We both thought we should try to do a bit on the ball ourselves, just to show that we could. I had a run and took on Purdy, the As' centre-back. I got the ball and I pushed it past him but he came after me and I back-heeled the ball into the space where Matty should have been running in, but he wasn't. Matty looked disgusted.

Wasted effort, and I'd made him look bad, without meaning to. If we'd known each other's style of play, it wouldn't have happened.

100

Alexiou had two runs, and each time Purdy kept me really closed down, and we couldn't work anything. Purdy was strong and sturdy, a really good player. That was the trouble with the whole game. *All* the players were good. Playing for Red Row, I could always count on being on-the-move before anybody else, but playing for the Bs I was shaded for speed because of my size. So I thought the best thing I could do was to play it simple and concentrate on drawing people on to me, then laying the ball off when my marker was committed. I started doing that but Purdy got wise to it. He didn't move into the tackle and I was left playing harmless balls outside with everyone covered.

'If you don't want to take him on, play it earlier to me,' Matty grunted.

I managed it the next time, and Matty got his shot in. McKee looked as if he had it covered and then his fingers went soapy. The ball ran loose. I closed in to score a Napper McCann Super Goal but I blasted it wide of the post, with the whole goal empty.

McKee stood there grinning at me. I'd let him off what would have been almost an own goal. The one good chance I was going to get, and I'd missed the kind of sitter nobody misses, not even Marky Bellow. All I'd had to do was to hit the ball straight.

'Lost your marker that time, any road!' Tom Brocken said to me encouragingly.

Then Matty got a goal.

It was soft.

Alexiou had played the ball through and McKee looked as if he had it covered and then he didn't come and Matty walked it round him.

The ball came down the field again, straight from the kick-off, just a big boot really, that wasn't going anywhere. McKee came out to gather it and he let it slither through his hands. Then he lunged back and knocked it sideways into Ronnie Purdy's path as the back ran in. It hit Purdy and dribbled on into the net. Ronnie Purdy was mad, and McKee was down in the mouth, looking as if he wanted the ground to swallow him.

It seemed to buck Purdy up. He got on top of me, and Alexiou and Matty were beginning to play between themselves, because I was out of it. I tried to push and run past Purdy, but I couldn't make it. He was too quick on the recovery.

I was bottled up.

Tom Brocken used his head. He could see what had happened to me. 'Play tap stuff with me,' he said, and that is what I did. The good thing was that he could really play, and he backed up every time I got near the ball, but the bad thing was that I didn't look good, and all the time Zan was making big runs down the other end, and getting our defence in a tangle.

Three times he got clear. Once he shot into the side netting and a second time he beat the back and Ally saved low at the post. The third time he beat three men all on his own but delayed his cross and Ally managed to come out and pluck the ball off Jezz's head. Jezz was mad, and yelled at Zan for delaying his cross and beating his man twice but Zan didn't seem to mind. He went on doing it.

Then Tom Brocken gave me the ball again and came pounding through for the return ball. I sensed Ronnie Purdy moving in anticipation that I'd pass back, and instead I dragged it like this, changing feet:

I was past Purdy, clean through, with McKee coming out at me.

BANG!

It hit McKee, and spun wildly up in the air but I was still going. I launched myself as it was coming down but McKee somehow doubled back in the air and clawed the ball off my head.

Another miss, with only the goalie to beat.

McKee was so pleased at making the save that he stood there congratulating himself. Then he dropped the ball to roll it out.

Matty was in like a flash!

G-o-a-l!

McKee just stood there with his hands on his hips, while we were all chasing big Matty up-field. It was a stupid goal to concede, but a great goal from Matty's point of view.

Then it was over.

Another game with no goals from N. McCann!

We were all in the dressing-room.

D. W. Ledley read out the Squad for the big game under floodlights at Owen Lane Stadium against Boyne Dynamo: Bantam, Brocken, Purdy, McCall, Usiskin, Reid, Alexiou, Matthews, Mole, McCann, Singh. Subs: Fish, Zan, Jezz, Bird, Scott.

McCann!

Me!

In the team!

I was in even though I hadn't scored!

I got my things on and floated out of the

dressing-room on to the coach! I couldn't wait to get home and tell them all. IN THE TEAM!

T. Cowans came and sat beside me.

'Well, pleased?' he said.

'Yeah!' I said.

'You nearly didn't make it, son,' he said. 'You have a problem, and we'll have to sort it out.'

I didn't say anything. My problem was being a Star Goalscorer who didn't score any goals.

'You know what you're doing?' he said. 'You're thinking too much.'

'Eh?' I said. I'd spent the first game working out that it was thinking players they were after, and now here he was telling me *not* to think.

'Just once in the second half you showed you had the beating of Ronnie Purdy. He's handy. He got on top of you early on. He was too quick on the turn for you, and he wouldn't come at you when you tried to draw him in. You let him force you into all that tip-tapping stuff with young Brocky. It was good stuff, but the defenders were reading it. But the one time you *forgot* he was bigger and faster than you and relied on your skill, you beat him all ends up. If you have the skill to do that once, you have the skill to do it again. You could have turned him inside out, I reckon . . . but you hadn't the confidence to do it. You thought you were bottled, and you took the easy option, playing tip-tap with Tom Brocken, or releasing the ball early to the big striker. You need to show us more of what you can really do on the ball if you are going to make it!'

'Y-E-S,' I said.

'I've only seen you play twice,' he said. 'Each time you've been worrying about the other players, because they were bigger and faster.'

'I'm more worried about not scoring any goals!' I said.

'The goals will come!' he said. 'You are looking for them, so that is no problem. You have a lot of skill, and you can spot an opening, but you are going to have to learn to take a few risks and go at people more.'

Then he went off.

Go at them!

That is what I do! I'd been doing it for ages, with Red Row, but the difference was that playing for them I expected to beat people, and I'd been put off by playing with better players, and spent too much time thinking about how good they were, and not how good I could be.

Right!

Don't *think* too much was the message . . .

Play your *own* game.

But . . . was my own game good enough?

The only place I could prove that was in the Big Match!

8. The Big Match

COMMUNITY CHALLENGE MATCH
Warne County Colts v. Boyne Dynamo
Referee: H. Hynes (County FA)
Venue: Owen Lane Stadium, Warne
(Under floodlights!)
In attendance: Almost everybody I know

I didn't know what it would be like. I thought it might feel the same as our League decider at Owen Lane, against St Gabriel's, but it wasn't.

There were lots more people there for a start. That was because our game was on before the T. Cowans Testimonial Game to show off the County's new Community Relations effort, and that meant a real football crowd in a real stadium under real floodlights.

When we ran out down the tunnel there were people cheering and lights in our eyes and a *funny* smell. I don't know why there should have been a special smell, but there was. It was like the smell of new grass, but all mixed up and *warmed*. I suppose that was because of the lights.

This is the way we lined up for the first-ever match played by Warne County Colts:

BANTAM
BROCKEN   PURDY   McCALL   USISKIN
ALEXIOU,   McCANN   REID   SINGH
MATTHEWS   MOLE
Subs: Fish, Zan, Jezz, Bird, Scott.

The trouble was we still didn't really *know* each other. We hadn't played together, and there had been no training sessions. D. W. Ledley muttered about that a bit, but it was because of the Building Society. They wanted our team to play before the Testimonial Match so that they would get lots of publicity, and G. Trotman and D. W. Ledley had had only a short time to find a team at all.

'Just go out there and do your best,' G. Trotman said, but D. W. Ledley wasn't leaving it like that. He came into the dressing-room and went round talking to everybody. He told me that Matty and Danny Mole would be the front runners and I was to play just behind them and feed off their knock-downs. Alexiou would be coming through from the midfield on the right, with Lester Singh using the left. Tom Brocken would be coming from the back and overlapping Alexiou because Tom is a big strong player and we thought he might be able to get some crosses in, and I was to link with him.

It was all a bit muddling.

I couldn't see how there'd be space on the right if Tom Brocken and Alexiou were both coming through, but they seemed to think they could work it out. I was to cover back if they went on runs, and that was what worried me. How could I cover back if I was supposed to be feeding off knock-downs from the big two in the middle? We would all be racing upfield and if it broke down there would be big gaps behind.

'You only cover back if they *both* go together,' D. W. Ledley said. 'Just keep your wits about you and you'll be all right.'

All *right* is just what I wouldn't be. There wasn't going to be any space on the right for me to move into, but that was what D. W. Ledley wanted us to do so I supposed we would have to do it. He said Joe Reid would cover for me and I was to keep an eye open for Lester Singh on the left because we knew Lester was the fastest player on the team and a sudden switched ball to him might put him clear.

'You feed *both* wings, Napper,' D. W. Ledley said, 'and you nip forward to the big two when you can.'

Now I was feeding both wings and nipping forward and covering back to link up with Brocken and that was all before we thought about *their* team at all. If their midfielder was any good, I knew I might spend all my time

109

closing him down, and then how could I do what D. W. Ledley wanted?

T. Cowans was in the dressing-room as well and he saw me looking grim when D. W. Ledley had moved on.

'Pay no heed, son,' he said. 'Davie Ledley likes to think he is coaching Brazil, not a team of schoolboys who have never played together before. Go out there and play your own game, and don't be afraid to take your man on.'

G-R-E-A-T! Now I was to make solo runs as well!

Then I was out on the field and it didn't seem to matter. There wasn't time to *think* any more, which was a good thing because *thinking* was giving me the shivers!

All I had to do was grab a goal or two! That was the important thing to remember! We had to line up in the middle of the field with Boyne Dynamo and then we were presented to the wife of the Chairman of the Brontley Building Society, and to T. Cowans, who was the player the Charity Game was for. It was his Benefit Match.

'Do your own thing, son,' he said, when he shook my hand.

I thought that was *probably* right, but I was worried by all D. W. Ledley's instructions. Then we had our photograph taken with the Building Society Placard:

110

SPONSORED BY
THE BRONTLEY BUILDING SOCIETY

'Remember I'm behind you, Napper,' Tom
Brocken said, when we were kicking in. Then
he went to the centre and tossed, and then we
kicked off.

All D. W. Ledley's lectures went out the
window.

Boyne Dynamo were greased lightning!

They had obviously played together as a
team, and they came at us straight from the
kick-off. Their left-winger kept going at Tom
and giving him a hard time and I found myself
drawn back, trying to keep the winger from
cutting inside.

111

Twice he beat both of us. The first time he put a high ball over and Tony Bantam came out of goal and took the ball off the striker's head, so that was all right. The next time he flicked past Tom and drew me on to the goal-line near the edge of the box and then he cut the ball back. Alexiou turned it round for a corner, with a diving header.

'Get your foot in, Napper!' D. W. Ledley barked at me from the touch-line.

If I'd got my foot in, it would have been a penalty, probably, so I thought that wasn't very smart.

'Close him down quicker if he goes by me, Napper,' Tom Brocken said.

The winger took the corner. It was a near-post ball and I started going for it but Tony Bantam came right through me without calling. I was knocked silly but he took the ball at full stretch. He threw it clear to Reid, who played it straight downfield to Big Matty. Matty took the ball on his chest and faked a turn so that his men went one way, and then he tapped it back . . . into the space where I *wasn't*, because I was still running out of the area.

'Faster, son!' D. W. Ledley bawled.

How could I have got it? I was being an emergency back, so how could I be upfield to take a lay-off? I haven't got magic legs.

They were back on the attack again. The

ball went down our right. I took the winger on. Tom laid off him and managed to nip it from him after he had rounded me, so that was all right. Tom gave me a short ball. I was coming off the winger and moving into their half with Alexiou outside me calling, so I slipped the ball to him and went right to overlap. Tom was going right too and we were both in the same space when the ball came. Tom took it because he was faster and he flighted a ball into the area but the goalie gathered it easily.

'*Inside* me, Napper,' Tom grunted.

I'd come across him and stopped his run. I should have been heading up the middle to be on the end of his cross.

The goalie's clearance came out and I went for it with a big Dynamo player called Yola or something like that. Maybe it was Yolande but that is a girl's name, and he wasn't a girl. He beat me to the ball but I doubled back and managed to cut out his pass inside. I played the ball square to Joe Reid and he got Singh away, but Lester put his head down and ran it over the goal-line.

The game began to settle. Ronnie Purdy and Nicky McCall were winning a lot of balls in midfield and Tom Brocken began to get a hold on the winger, so that was sorted out, and I was able to start moving forward more.

Big Matty and Danny Mole were holding their

own in the middle, but so far I hadn't been able to get on the end of anything. They were shouting at me to find space behind them, so it wasn't looking good for me although the team was doing well. All I had done so far was to play a few one-twos with Tom Brocken and one solitary through ball to Matty when he had moved over to the right, but I couldn't seem to find Danny Mole at all and twice when Alexiou cut in across the defenders I had missed him. Lester Singh, out on the wing, was left looking lonely and fed up, because no one was feeding him passes. It wasn't easy. Playing for Red Row I'd been used to having big gaps to move into because some of the players I was against were no good, but the Dynamo players were well drilled. It wasn't that they were so much better than our team, it was just that they knew each other. When one of them went up, another one covered back automatically. Being smaller than most of them didn't help me either. It meant that I lost two out of three balls against Yola, who was the player I was immediately up against. He was buffeting me about every time we went for the ball.

'Sort him!' Danny Mole said to me. 'He'll have you out of the game if you don't.' Danny was growing impatient with me because I was supposed to feed him, and nothing was coming through from me at all.

It was all very well for Danny to shout at me,

114

I didn't know how to sort him! I was afraid that if Yola got on top of me I would be substituted at half-time and they would bring on Zan or Jezz, who could both play a bit.

Then the winger got away from Tom Brocken and turned Alexiou who'd been covering back. He was clear in the area and Ronnie Purdy came across and crash-tackled him. It was a penalty, and a yellow card for Ronnie that *might* have been a red one, so really he was lucky.

Tony was bouncing up and down on his line, and we all lined up for their player to take the kick.

I remembered what we used to do at Red Row when there was a penalty, and I stayed back, just to the left of the kicker, but about five metres behind. The penalty taker started his run.

When he was three or four strides from the ball, I started mine so that I was just outside the area as he made contact.

WHAM!

It was a great shot.

I don't know how Tony even got near to it, but he did. He went left and stuck out his hand and the ball came back. I was going for it *first* because I'd been moving when the ball was struck.

I wasn't the only one.

Yola was after it too. He went past me and I stuck out my foot and I got a nick on the ball and . . .

G-o-a-l!

Own goal.

No goals at all for ages . . . and now I had scored one for the other team!

All the Dynamo players were going mad and their supporters were dancing about and I was left lying there, looking at the ball where I had placed it, just the wrong side of the post, in our net.

Ronnie Purdy was standing with his head in his hands.

Tom came over, and heaved me up.

'Tough,' he said.

It seemed a long, long way back to the centre circle for the restart.

G. Trotman cupped his hands and yelled at me from the dug-out.

'Now do it the other end, son.'

0–1 down in our Big Match!

Then the loudspeakers said: 'First goal. Thirty-two minutes, twenty-three seconds. Number 10. O.G.'

O.G.

Own Goal.

My first goal in a black and white Warne County jersey, and it was for the other team.

I thought I would get down to the other end and score one back, just to show I could do it, but every time I got the ball big Yola bundled me off it. There seemed to be nothing I could do but lay it off, and even that didn't seem to go right, because Danny Mole was pulling back from the centre to try and help me and that left Matty bottled up, and Lester Singh standing all on his own. Alexiou was doing what he could, but he couldn't make much of an impression on their defence without back up.

Half-time.

I thought it was probably full time as far as I was concerned, because I had done almost nothing except score an own goal and the man I was up against, Yola, was running the middle of the field. I thought I would be o-u-t, and one of the subs would be on. I was really disgusted.

We went down to the dressing-room under the stands. Everybody slumped down in the seats and then D. W. Ledley came in on his own, and closed the door firmly behind him.

'Well done, lads,' he said. 'Good game so far.'

'They're all over us, Mr Ledley,' Lester muttered.

'Yes, well, it is time you got moving, son, and did something about it,' Mr Ledley said. 'In

the Trial matches, you were the fastest thing on the park. You are supposed to be going at them wide down the left, but half the time you are out of it, and when you do get the ball you've been coming inside. Am I right?'

Lester just nodded, and started looking at his boots.

'Am I right, Singhy?' Mr Ledley barked.

'Not getting the ball, am I?' Lester said. 'No support from the back.'

That meant *me*. Well, me and Nicky McCall. Wally Usiskin was lying back, and Alexiou was going wide on the right, and McCall and I were supposed to be getting Lester Singh wide, but we hadn't been doing it.

'Show yourself to them, Singhy,' Mr Ledley said. 'I didn't hear you call once!'

Then he started on the defence.

'You are letting them settle on the ball,' he said. 'You have got to tighten it up. Our midfield haven't a chance, because they are covering back for you all the time. Start getting the tackles in *outside* the box, eh, Ronnie?'

Ronnie Purdy sniffed.

'You and Tom Brocken are supposed to be our ball-winners! Win it!'

Then he started on *us*.

'McCann . . . the big lad in the middle is taking you out of the game. The Number 6, right? I want you off him. Danny Mole . . . you

119

switch with Napper for the first ten minutes.
Stand on the Number 6. If he falls apart, they'll
fall apart. See how it goes. If that doesn't work,
switch back, and we'll try something else.
Alexiou . . . remember the Trial game? You and
Napper. We thought . . . two little blokes, and
they are getting together, they're moving. But
you're not, either of you! Napper has been
rubbed out and you are not showing, and the
result is no ball for the two front runners! I
want you to run the legs off them with through-
balls, feed the middle.'

I looked at Alexiou. That wasn't what they'd
told us. We were supposed to be doing pretty
patterns on the right, with Tom Brocken, and
drawing the defenders in so that Lester Singh
would get clear runs on the left when we could
find him.

'That's not what you told us before the game,'
Alexiou said. I thought it was brave of him to
speak out. I wouldn't have risked it, not at half-
time in our first big game.

'Look, son,' D. W. Ledley said. 'Why do you
think you are out there, and not some of the
others? We picked this whole team on the
grounds that the players could play, whatever
situation they were in. Difference between a
good player and a bad one. A bad one can only
play one way, and he keeps on doing it. You
and Napper McCann both showed in the Trials

120

that you could spot what was going on around you, and adjust to it. What I told you to do *isn't* working, right? If it doesn't work, what do you do?'

'Try something else,' Alexiou said.

'Right! Go out and do it! Danny Mole will take Yola out, Napper will nip about up front instead of *napping*, and you can up your work-rate a bit too, instead of fading out on the right.'

Then it was time to go back up the tunnel on to the pitch, for the second half.

I knew I'd done nothing in the first, so it was make or break time!

9. Second Half

We came out of the tunnel still stinging a bit over what D. W. Ledley had said. I hadn't been *napping*, and Alexiou hadn't been fading out. It was just that Yola had got on top of me, and Alexiou had no one to play to, which left Danny Mole standing up front looking rather silly, and Lester Singh with no ball to play with.

'If he could see it happening, why didn't he do something about it?' I said to Tom Brocken as we came out on to the pitch. Then I thought a bit more. D. W. Ledley was in the dug-out, not on the pitch. Once we were out there, we had to do it *ourselves*.

Danny Mole went on Yola, in my position, and that left me playing up front, with Singhy outside me, and Big Matty to my right. I was hoping that the Number 4, who would be marking me, wouldn't be as sharp as Yola.

I got my first touch.

Matty had crossed over to my left and he headed the ball right, so that it fell in my path.

I was going to lay it wide for Alexiou but then somebody yelled, out on the left. It was Lester Singh coming alive at last!

I hit a through ball, inside the back.

Lester got the ball, took it to the line and crossed, pulling the ball back for me to net it. I got up to it, and headed . . . just over.

Another miss!

'That's it, Napper!' Matty said, grinning at me.

'Keep doing it!' Ronnie Purdy said to me, as we were trotting back. 'You owe me one!' He was still down in the dumps, because he had given away the penalty that led to the goal . . . my own goal.

Then:

'What are you doing back here?' Tom Brocken said to me, and I realized I'd moved out to cover him, when I was supposed to be up front, playing with Matty.

The next time Alexiou got the ball, he played a neat pass to me right on the edge of the area and I played it into Tom Brocken's path. Tom got to the byline and switched it inside and there was Matty rising like a bird to nod it in.

G-O-A-L!

1–1.

As Alexiou played the ball to me he had taken his marker inside, making room for Tom Brocken's run from the back. It was simple and neat, and almost exactly what we had been supposed to do in the first half. It hadn't worked then because I had been caught up in my battle with Yola, but now Danny Mole was tussling with him, and I had more room to play. I was pleased, because I had been part of the build-up, but it still didn't make up for the O.G.

Things began to turn round for us, and all because of the one change, bringing Danny Mole back and switching me forward. Danny had been isolated up front, and now he was taking over the middle. I'd been lost against big Yola, but I had the beating of the Number 4. Up till then, like Danny, he had had nothing to do, and suddenly I was running him all over the park!

With Danny winning the ball against Yola, we were able to feed Lester Singh, and for the first time he began going at his man, with space to move in. I kept switching with Matty, and throwing their centre into confusion. Lester was flighting the ball over, and making things happen in their box. Even Ronnie Purdy was able to make a few runs forward, interchanging with McCall.

Then Danny put me clear down the middle and I drew the Number 5 and made as if to pass to Matty, putting the Number 5 off balance. Instead of passing I nicked it past the defender on the inside and closed in on the keeper, before pushing the ball square, right into Matty's path, leaving the keeper stranded. Matty walked it into the net.

GOAL!

It *might* not have counted, because Lester Singh had run offside, anticipating that I would play it wide, but either the referee didn't spot it or he ruled that Lester wasn't interfering with play. I think Lester was, because the goalie must have been aware that he was there, on the outside, but the referee gave a goal, so that was it.

2–1 to Warne County Colts and suddenly we were all over them. Singhy was outpacing his man and big Matty was on a hat trick and I was doing one-twos with Alexiou and Danny Mole was linking with us and doing runs of his own. We seemed to have the game all sewn up, except for getting goals! It was all action attack.

WHAM from Ronnie Purdy, almost twenty metres out, and their goalie saved it at the post.

Then the goalie did it again, smothering the ball at big Matty's feet. Then Alexiou broke down the right and slung one across and I was coming in and . . .

Zammooo!
Goal! Goal! Goal!
A Napper McCann Super Goal on my début for the team, a flying Wham-Bam header from the edge of the goalie's box.

Offside!

I stood gaping at the ref. I couldn't understand it. How could I be offside? The ball was in the net and it was a Napper McCann Super Goal and I'd come from behind the ball, so I couldn't be offside.

'Och, ref!' Danny Mole yelled and he was booked.

Then the ref gave the free kick out on the left . . . so I wasn't offside, it was Singhy again. The trouble was that Lester Singh was so fast that he kept moving into offside positions.

'Watch it, son!' D. W. Ledley yelled at him from the dug-out.

Then Yola got free of Danny for once, and Ronnie Purdy got to him and brought him down. It was a bad tackle, and Ronnie already had a yellow card from the first half. I thought he might be sent off, but he got a talking-to instead.

The trainer came on for Yola.

'Napper!' T. Cowans came from the dug-out.

'Yes?'

'Do a wee bit, Napper! Do it on the ball.'

So I did.

And it worked.

I skinned the Number 4 twice.

The first time I turned inside him and got the ball to big Matty, who missed, and the second time I went outside him and got inside the box. Yola came crunching in but I rode his tackle and got a thumping shot in at the near post but the goalie smothered it.

'Lester was free!' D. W. Ledley yelled at me.

'Sorry, Lester,' I said, but Lester just grinned at me. 'You beat him,' he said. 'Keep doing it.'

The Dynamo manager was up off the bench yelling too, and the next thing I knew the Number 4 had come off me and Yola was pulled back to do it.

I thought I could turn him inside out, now that I had my confidence back, but it didn't work out that way. I tried him three times, but I couldn't get past him, and I was left tip-tapping again, but the good thing was that it stopped Yola going forward and suddenly Danny Mole was doing what I was supposed to do in the first half.

Yola was really mad. He couldn't be every-where at once, and the rest of the Dynamo back four couldn't cope with Danny spraying the ball about and Lester Singh running at them.

We were right on top.

Lester got clear, put his head down as usual, and blazed the ball wide, just as Yola tackled him.

Then Yola turned a shot from Matty over the bar, with his keeper beaten.

Then it was my turn again, taking Yola on for a high centre. I couldn't beat him in the air but I did enough to put him off. Danny got the loose ball, following up, and really banged it. It hit their back, standing on the line, and Yola got it clear.

Brocken came up to me.

'Go wide,' he said.

'Why?' I said. 'It is working the way it is.'

'Try it,' he said.

And I did.

And it was even *better*.

When I went wide, Yola had to go with me, and that took him out of the centre of their defence. Lester Singh switched sides with Alexiou and suddenly he was running at the Number 3, who couldn't take him.

Then Danny had a shot at goal that was blocked on the line and I nearly got it but Yola put his foot in the way and it went for a corner.

The corner came over and Matty got up above everybody and powered his header in. The ball hit the bar and came down and Alexiou hit it point blank at the goal. It bounced off their back, who was standing on the line, and cannoned into the goalie's arms.

The crowd were going wild.

The goalie threw the ball downfield, to their centre-forward.

We were all up, except Ronnie Purdy.

Ronnie went for him with one of his slide-tackles, and missed. Ronnie was lucky that he did miss, because if he had got the tackle in, he would have been sent off for deliberately bringing down a man who was clear.

Their centre drew Tony from his goal, and then he chipped the ball.

Goal.

D. W. Ledley had his head in his hands.

G. Trotman just stood there, glowering at Ronnie.

Ronnie got up, with a long face. If he had stayed on his feet and not lunged at the striker he might have been able to do something, but by committing himself to the late tackle he had left the way clear to goal.

I felt really sorry for him. He was the strong man in our defence and he'd been cutting everything out, but he had given away the penalty that led to the first goal, and now he was going to be blamed for the second. It was hard luck, and it only happened because he was the quickest and strongest of our defenders, the one who managed to be there when it came to the important tackles, so it was the sort of thing that always could happen to him. He'd played much better than some of the others, Reidy and old Wally Usiskin for instance, but they were let off the hook because he had made the big mistakes.

We were all to blame, really. We'd gone mad in attack, trying to seal the game, and so we deserved to be caught on the break.

Warne County Colts 2–Boyne Dynamo 2.

I thought I would get a great breakthrough in the last minute and score the winning goal that would decide the match, but I didn't.

Yola didn't let me.

He didn't let up at all. I was aching because

131

of the banging he'd been giving me and the best I managed before the end was to slip him once and play the ball through for Lester, who was offside again.

The whistle blew. 2–2.

A draw, when we wanted to win it, because it was our very first big game under Warne County floodlights with a big crowd. We had taken Boyne Dynamo on and sorted them out, but we had thrown it away.

Then G. Trotman and the Dynamo Manager came on to the pitch and talked to the ref.

D. W. Ledley came over to our team and he said, 'Right. Who is taking the penalties?'

It was Tom Brocken and Ronnie and Matty and Danny Mole – and big Usiskin, who had hardly been in the match at all but D. W. Ledley seemed to think he could do it.

I lay on the grass, exhausted.

I should have been one of the penalty takers.

Scoring goals is what I do . . . but I had been missing them all along the line. I couldn't blame D. W. Ledley for not picking me, but that didn't stop it feeling rotten!

Dynamo took the first one and scored.

Tom Brocken took ours. He nearly broke the net!

1–1.

Dynamo again. Tony got a hand to the ball, and turned it on to the upright, but it ended up in the net. 2–1 to Dynamo.

Ronnie Purdy was next. He was really cool about it, and the Dynamo keeper never even sniffed it.

2–2.

Yola took the third one for Dynamo. This time Tony got it! It was a full-length save at the bottom left-hand corner. Yola went down on his knees, pounding the ground.

Matty. Bang! Matty did a wild dance round the area till the ref stopped him!

2–3 to us! We were winning because of Tony's Super Save!

Tony looked very confident lining up for Dynamo's fourth penalty. He went right, and the Dynamo player's shot went left! 3–3!

Then Danny Mole missed!

Dynamo went mad! They'd been out of it, and now they stood a chance again, with just one shot each to go!

The Dynamo player who had to take the next one looked really nervous, and he looked even worse when Tony stuck out his knee and stopped his shot.

We were all dancing about.

It was still 3–3, with our last penalty to come. If Usiskin scored, we had won!

I could hardly look! I felt sorry for Usiskin. He had hardly figured in the match at all. I don't know why he got to take the penalty. It should have been me, but it wasn't, because I had done nothing but miss chances during all the games D. W. Ledley had seen me play in.

Usiskin took his time placing the ball. He was pale and nervous-looking, but he hit a good shot, low down for the bottom corner. He should have scored, but he didn't. The keeper got down and turned it against the post, and this time the ball came back, instead of banging into the net.

3–3!

We had let it slip when we could have won! Sudden death!

Dynamo had the first sudden-death penalty, and Tony could do nothing about it. D. W. Ledley talked to G. Trotman, and then he handed the ball to Lester Singh.

Lester placed it, and walked back. Then he ran up and smashed it home!

4–4!

Tony took his time, walking to the goal for the next one.

He crouched on the line and the Dyamo

player ran up and hit the ball about three trillion miles over the bar, right into the crowd!

Our chance to win it!

And D. W. Ledley chucked the ball to me!

'You keep talking about being a striker, son,' he said. 'Now you've got your chance!'

I put the ball on the spot.

Then I walked back.

I was trying to think that it was just another spot-kick, it didn't matter, and then I knew it wasn't. It was the one chance I had to show them that I could do what I am supposed to be able to do. Score goals.

So I *had* to score.

No putting it through the goalie's legs this time, because the Dynamo goalie wasn't going to do a Dicey and let me get away with a silly trick like that. I made up my mind where I was putting it.

Inside the left-hand post, just out of the keeper's reach, that was what I decided.

And . . .

That was what I did!

GOAL! Goal! Goal! Goal! G-o-a-l!

A Napper McCann Super Goal at last! At least, it felt like a Super Goal, even though it was only a penalty. I didn't care! Any goal would have done!

4–5! We had won on penalties! D. W. Ledley and G. Trotman were up off the bench congratulating us and we were going off the pitch and everyone was cheering and . . .

. . . it was over.

Finished.

But not *finished*.

Only beginning, really.

It was an odd feeling, leaving the dressing-room after the game and knowing that next week we'd be back training and we would really become a team, Warne County Colts, and there would be lots of games and we might win cups and medals and tournaments.

It should have been brilliant and exciting and the Greatest Ever and in a way it was, but in another way it wasn't. I felt tired out. I just couldn't take any more. Maybe it was too exciting. I'd played in the game and I'd scored the winning goal and it was like something in a silly comic plot only it wasn't in a comic, it was real!

Daniel was waiting for me at the Players' Entrance.

He started cheering and shouting when he saw me coming and I felt really odd, out of it, almost embarrassed. My dad was there, and so were the last people I had expected to see – Mr Hope and Miss Fellows! They were patting me on the back and saying how brilliant I was and what a good game it had been, and I couldn't say anything.

'Well done, Napper,' Mr Hope said. 'See you at school, Monday!' and off he went.

'He looks really pleased,' Daniel said.

'So he should,' my dad said. 'He's the one who recommended Napper to the club, isn't he?'

'Eh?' I said, totally surprised.

'Doesn't do any harm you knowing now, Napper,' my dad said. 'Mr Hope came to see me at the start of the term, when he found out it wasn't going to be possible to have a school team. He said he'd try to get you fixed up. And that was what he did.'

'But ... but he tried to stop me playing!' I said. 'He wasn't going to let me go for the Final Trial.'

'Is that what you really think?' Dad said. 'Head teachers have to stick together, you know!'

Mr Hope *hadn't* tried to stop me playing. He'd found me a team without even telling me.

'Mr Hope got you your chance!' Dad said.

'Yes. But Napper took it!' Daniel said.

I DID.

He was right.

Napper McCann, Super Star, was back on the Goal Trail!

NAPPER GOES FOR GOAL
Martin Waddell

Napper McCann and the star players of Red Row Primary School start a football team and imagine a glorious, successful future. But then they discover how hard it is to win games. A funny and exciting story with plenty of illustrations and diagrams for football fans.

THE BEST-KEPT SECRET
Emily Rodda

The arrival of the fairground carousel, surrounded by its neat red and white painted fence, with a tent guarding its entrance, was a complete mystery to the residents of Marley Street. Where had it come from? How had it appeared so quickly? And why was the music so haunting, beckoning all to come and look? Jo is determined to have a ride, even though she senses the ride may take her into danger, into an unknown world ... the world of the future.

SKYLARK
K. M. Peyton

Life isn't much fun for Ben – until he meets Elf and is drawn into an exciting adventure. But the two children must keep their secret from the thoughtless adults in this delightful and touching story. He wished he was brave, like boys in books, but the fact was ... he was hating every minute of his adventure.

THE CURSE OF HACKJAW ISLAND
Scoular Anderson

Take one crazy cook, two young orphans, a miserable ghost, a talking skull, a team of rats, some bumbling pirates and two lots of treasure and what have you got?

The Curse of Hackjaw Island!

It's the funniest, craziest, zaniest, most riotous pirate romp around. But BEWARE. Do not read it while walking along a plank as you may laugh yourself off the edge!

MUM'S WINNING STREAK
David Wiseman

Angie and her dad get used to having pears instead of mushy peas because Mum's taken the labels off the tins to enter another competition, and Goliath, the monster cat brought in to eat their year's free supply of cat food, becomes one of the family. But Wallace Windle is something else. Dinner for Mum with her favourite film star turns into a nightmare as Wallace moves in and makes everyone's life a misery.

A quite hilarious story. Read it, and you'll never enter a competition again!